CHAMPION OF FREEDOM

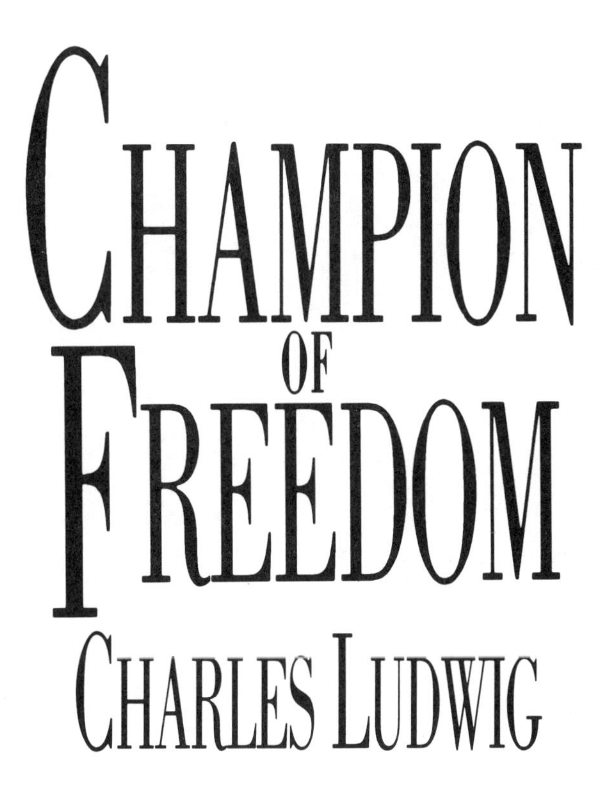

CHAMPION OF FREEDOM

CHARLES LUDWIG

BETHANY HOUSE PUBLISHERS
MINNEAPOLIS, MINNESOTA 55438
A Division of Bethany Fellowship, Inc.

Published by Bethany House Publishers
A Division of Bethany Fellowship, Inc.
6820 Auto Club Road, Minneapolis, Minnesota 55438

Printed in the United States of America

Library of Congress Cataloging-in-Publication Data

Ludwig, Charles, 1918–
Champion of freedom.

1. Stowe, Harriet Beecher, 1811–1896, in fiction, drama, poetry, etc. I. Title.
PS3523.U434C5 1987 813'.52 87–20884
ISBN 0–87123–965–5

To the memory of "Auntie" Elizabeth Hetrick, my parents' housekeeper who helped raise me. When I was eight she kept me spellbound as she read *Uncle Tom's Cabin.* A year later, she inspired me to make my life count by pointing out a sculpture of Harriet Beecher Stowe in New York City's Hall of Fame.

About the Author

Author Charles Ludwig grew up on the mission field in Kenya. He brings to his third historical novel with BHP an impressive writing experience, having more than forty books already published, several of which have been read or dramatized on worldwide radio. Ludwig also has a rich pastoral and evangelistic ministry, having preached across Europe and in many other countries. He and his wife make their home in Tucson, Arizona.

Other Biographical Novels

Queen of the Reformation—Katie Luther
Mother of an Army—Catherine Booth

Acknowledgments

From the time Harriet Beecher Stowe's *Uncle Tom's Cabin* was read to me when I was eight, I've been interested in the author, wanting to know how such a tiny fragment of humanity was able to stir the world. Following my fascination, I visited Litchfield where she was born and where her father preached. Then I went to Brunswick, Maine, where Harriet Stowe had a "vision" of Uncle Tom—and there wrote the book.

Intrigued by Tom and Eliza, my wife and I photographed the famous John Rankin House in Ripley, Ohio. Perched on a cliff overlooking the broad Ohio River, this preacher-house was a stopping place on the Underground Railroad. It was from this residence that help was extended to Eliza after she had managed to leap from one cake of ice to another in her escape. It was also near this house, during a minister's convention, that Harriet began her romance with Calvin Stowe.

Crossing into Kentucky, Mary and I drove to the plantation that had allegedly belonged to Simon Legree—the man who owned Uncle Tom. We also stopped at the nearby cemetery where, according to legend, Legree is buried. Legend also insists that on three occasions lightning shattered the slab of cement over his grave.

In gathering material, I've used many books, both from the University of Arizona, and the Huntington Library in San Marino, California, which contains the largest collection of Harriet Beecher Stowe material in America.

Miss Sue Hodson, the Curator of the Harriet Beecher Stowe collection, was most helpful, as were all the other members of the staff.

How much of this book is true? I did take the liberty to name two of the many cats at the Beecher home in Litchfield, and I invented one character, the former slave, Sam. Otherwise, all the other names and events are actual.

I must also extend my thanks to the editors at Bethany House Publishers for their interest in publishing this work.

Table of Contents

Acknowledgments 7
Preface 11
1. Litchfield 13
2. The Fourth 21
3. Sorrow 31
4. New Worlds 44
5. A Churning World 51
6. The New Flower 62
7. Darkness at High Noon 70
8. Boston 78
9. A Dog, A Petticoat, and Two Lanterns 86
10. Trapped! 98
11. The Lure of the West 107
12. Cincinnati 117
13. Semi-Colon Club 125
14. The Underground Railroad 134
15. Romance! 143
16. Trail of Tears 154
17. Purgatory 163
18. The Vision 173
19. Uncle Tom 182
20. Grapes of Wrath 194
21. Emancipation Proclamation 205
22. Epilogue 212
Appendix 217
Chronology 218
Bibliography 220

Preface

Congressman Philip Greeley of Boston settled himself in the night train for New York and Washington. Then to pass the time, he began to read volume one of the cloth-bound book just presented to him by Professor Calvin Stowe.

Although he had not read any of the story as it was being published in serial form in the *National Era*, he halfway expected to be bored. Indeed, when the publisher, fearing its failure, had offered to share the profits if Calvin would put up half the money, Greeley had advised against it. A ten percent royalty, he was convinced, was a much better proposition for the over-lengthy novel.

Opening to the first page, the Congressman began to read: "Late in the afternoon of a chilly day in February, two gentlemen were sitting alone over their wine in a well-furnished dining parlor in the town of P——, in Kentucky." Soon the book became alive. The rhythmic beating of the carriage wheels retreated into silence. The pages quickly shuffled beneath his eager fingers. He became conscious of tears coursing down his cheeks and of people staring curiously at him. But in spite of the scene he was creating, he could not lay the book down. In desperation he got off the train at Springfield, checked into a hotel and wept his way through both volumes.

Uncle Tom's Cabin, by Harriet Beecher Stowe, was on its way! Soon the presses were rumbling day and night. Twenty thousand copies were sold in three weeks alone. This was the mere beginning. It was translated into one language after another. It became an instant hit on Broadway. It was pirated in England. More importantly, it became the leading cause for the abolition of slavery.

No one was more astonished by this success than the author. After the contract had been signed, she timidly remarked, "I hope it earns enough money so that I may have a silk dress."

To an admirer she replied with typical modesty, "I am a little bit of a woman—about as thin and dry as a pinch of snuff."

All eleven of Lyman Beecher's children made an impact with their lives. His seven sons were preachers. Catherine won renown as a pioneer in women's education. Isabella etched her mark as a suffragette, Mary became the wife of a leading attorney. And Harriet blossomed into one of the world's most famous authors.

Busts of both Harriet and Henry Ward are in the Hall of Fame.

So successful was this family that Theodore Parker declared: "Lyman Beecher was the father of more brains than any other man in America." And Dr. Leonard Bacon of New Haven commented that America is "inhabited by saints, sinners, and Beechers."

Both men were right. And even though Lyman's mother died at his premature birth, he possessed a secret: He *expected* his children to succeed—and raised them in a Christian atmosphere.

1

Litchfield

Harriet rubbed her eyes, stumbling toward the kitchen. She had no idea that she would grow up to become the most famous author in America, and that she would write a book that would help free millions of slaves. Nor did she understand that her father had a unique way of raising children, a way that would help make all of them useful—and several of them famous. The one thing she understood was that she had been awakened by the tangy aroma of bacon.

Bacon and eggs meant dawn. Dawn meant that it was time for all the Beechers in Litchfield to get up and start changing the world.

"Breakfast's 'bout ready," announced Zillah, one of the two black teenagers in charge of the kitchen. Skillfully Zillah broke more eggs on the edge of the skillet. While they bubbled and spat, she added, "Better wake your pa while the food's hot."

Complying with a squeal of delight, Harriet barged into her father's room. Waking him on Monday morning was almost as exciting as watching the parades on the Fourth of July. This morning she had no idea that she was gaining experience for a time nearly a half century later when she would call on a former rail-splitter and urge him to issue the Emancipation Proclamation. "Pa," she squeaked, "bwakefast's almost weady."

Lyman Beecher did not respond.

Harriet raised her voice. "Git up, Papa!"

No answer.

"Git up! Git up! Git up!" she sang.

America's most distinguished preacher refused to budge. Desperately Harriet peeled a corner of the covers from his face. Then, while pinching the end of his nose, she repeated, "Bwakefast is almost weady."

The sleepy man pushed out his big toe.

Encouraged, Harriet climbed down off the big bed and started to leave. She had just reached the door when he groaned and jerked his toe back to safety under the covers. "I can't get up. I can't get up." His voice shuddered with terror.

"Why not?" Harriet grinned, for this answer was part of the routine.

"B-b-because there's a hungry lion under the b-b-bed."

"There's no lion under the bed," assured Harriet.

"A-are you sure?"

"Papa, I'm sure."

"Maybe you'd better crawl under the bed and make sure. I d-don't relish being e-eaten—especially this early in the morning." Shuddering at this imminent possibility, he crunched even deeper into the bed.

Thoughtfully, Harriet paused with her hand on the doorknob. The smells of breakfast were becoming more tantalizing, and since they were required to have family worship *before* they could eat, she realized that she needed help. Knowing she'd have to crawl under the bed, search out the closet, look behind the cupboard, and examine all the corners before her father would get up, there was only one answer.

Stepping out the door, she called for her six-year-old brother George, and her ten-year-old sister Mary. Following her directions, they finally assured America's most noted theologian that there were no lions or even tigers in his room. Bouncing out of bed, he inwardly rejoiced in knowing that he had helped sharpen his children's imagination.

Following worship, all eight Beecher children, their mother Roxana, the three boarders who attended Sarah Pierce's school for young ladies, Betsy Burr, the orphan cousin of Lyman's assistant Mr. Cornelius, along with several guests, took their places at the enormous table.

After grace, and after he had eaten several eggs and a few pieces of bacon, Lyman Beecher began to reminisce. "As most of you know, my first church was in East Hampton, Long Island. The first pastor received one fourth of the whales stranded on the beach, was allowed to be first in line to have his grain ground, did not have to pay taxes on his land—and was paid forty-five pounds a year.

"I didn't fare so well. I only received four hundred dollars a year and firewood. Roxana had to open a school." He exchanged glances with his wife.

"Here, I get twice as much money. And they bring my firewood. But when they bring it they cause a big problem for me." Frowning, he helped himself to another egg and some fried potatoes.

"When they bring the wood, they're not careful about where they drop it. Now, as you know I've been in a contest with the president of Yale. Doctor Taylor thinks he can raise cucumbers faster than I can. He can't. I always have more and bigger cucumbers than he has, and I have them on the table before he does." He nodded assuringly.

"I have a secret." My secret is that I start my cucumbers in cold frames. The frames protect them from the frost. But now my friends have piled wood on those frames." He shook his head sorrowfully. "This means I'll need your help to move the firewood . . ."

Roxana neither smiled nor frowned, for she realized that Lyman was far more interested in raising useful children than in producing cucumbers; and that he had a subtle way of teaching them without their knowledge. Experience had taught her to conceal this understanding.

Since everyone was eager to help, the preacher continued eating in silence. Then his eyes lit up. "I really enjoyed preaching yesterday," he confessed. "God *is* sovereign! Still, I believe in free will. Those opposites cling together like bacon and eggs. It's as Jonathan Edward says: you cannot have light without heat." Carried away, he thumped the table with such force the knives and forks jumped. "Had not Moses *obeyed* God, His providence would not have separated the Red Sea. . . .

"God hates dueling. But His providence cannot stop this type of murder until *we* do something about it. That's the reason God directed me to preach my sermon against dueling. Forty thousand copies of that sermon were distributed! In time God's providence will put an end to dueling . . ."

Annoyed that few were listening, he pointed to Harriet. "Hattie listened more closely than any of you. Her eyes never moved from the pulpit. And she's only four!"

The rest of the children glanced at Harriet and then down at their plates. The silence was finally broken by Roxana: "Catherine has a poem we ought to hear. It might inspire us to put an end to one of our worst problems—"

"What's it about?" asked Harriet, bursting with pride.
"Rats," replied Roxana.
"Rats?" questioned Mary.
"Yes, rats!" confirmed their mother.
"All right, let's hear about the rats," nodded Lyman, exerting his authority as head of the house.

Standing in front of her empty plate, Catherine, the oldest of the Beecher children, cleared her throat and read from the back of the envelope in her hand:

One rat slipped on Miss Katy's shoes
And danced about the room
While with tongs and candlestick
Two others kept the tune.

One rat jumped onto Harriet's bed
And began to gnaw her nose.
The other chose another extreme
And nibbled Mary's toes—[1]

After the clapping, Roxana said, "Lyman, we must do something about those rats!"

"Any suggestions? We already have a dozen cats."

"I'll tell you what I think we should do," Roxana laced her voice with authority. "We should stop feeding them! Look at Thomas Junior. He's so full of bacon and eggs all he can do is sit and scrub his whiskers."

Unconcerned that he was the center of attention, the black tomcat continued to preen, his pink tongue moving in and out as he licked his paw and carefully polished his face.

"He could at least frighten a few mice if he ever got hungry," added Roxana. "I doubt if he's even tried to catch the tiniest mouse. But why should he? Look at his plate! It's nearly full. Soon he'll be so fat he'll begin to stagger . . ."

"Maybe so," Lyman chuckled. "But in the meantime it's time to move that firewood. Catherine will be leaving for school in less than an hour, so let's get busy."

It had always bothered Harriet that her father wished she were a boy. Now, deciding to please him, she wrapped up in one of Edward's outgrown coats. She had just started for the woodpile when her father, not noticing how she was dressed, commented, "Hattie, I've lost my hat."

Since the preacher lost his hat almost every day, Hattie had become an expert at finding it. If it wasn't by the fire-

[1]*The Beechers*, by Milton Rugoff, p. 42.

place, it was generally near the big chair where he liked to study. Having located the hat, Harriet gave it to her father. Beecher stuffed it on his head and began to show the children just how the wood was to be moved and stacked.

As saws cut and axes chopped, Lyman watched. Then, as he helped with his own axe, he said between puffs, "I'm the happiest man—in the world. I have—the best family—in the world; and I—have the best church—in the world."

"Pa, a-are we better than Piskerpalians and Lutherans and Baptists?" asked Harriet.

"Of course not. But the Congregationalists or Presbyterians *are* the Established Church in New England." Placing the log he had just severed onto the woodpile, he continued. "Like all the other Footes, your mother was an Episcopalian before I married her. And so is her grandfather, General Ward.

"You see, Hattie, during the Revolution George III was the head of the Church of England. That's what they call the Episcopalians over there. Since he was our enemy, some Colonists tore down his statue in Bowling Green and dumped it in Litchfield. It was melted and molded into 42,088 bullets."

"But I like the Piskerpalians," argued Harriet.

"The word is Episcopalians," corrected Beecher. "Why do you like them?" He began to shorten another log.

"Because they celebrate Christmas. Catherine and I peeked through the windows of their church last December. It was full of flowers and there was a tall tree in front and it was lit with candles. Papa, you should have heard them sing! Can't we celebrate Christmas?"

"We celebrate the Fourth of July and Thanksgiving. Isn't that enough?"

"Maybe," replied Harriet thoughtfully. "Still, I like Christmas." Suddenly she changed the subject. "Papa, why did you want me to be a boy?"

Lyman leaned on his ax. "I like girls, Harriet," he said, smiling at her. "But I'm especially fond of boys because they can become Congregational or Presbyterian preachers. Preachers, Hattie, can change the world and help bring the millennium. So far, I have five sons—preachers-to-be. William Henry, Edward, George, Henry Ward, and Charles.

"But, Hattie, I love you very much. We named you after the first Harriet. She only lived about a month."

"I know all about it," acknowledged Harriet. "Catherine told me." Then she asked another question, totally unrelated to the present subject. "Pa, why did you tell Judge Reeve that although I wasn't very p-r-e-t-t-y, I was very s-m-a-r-t?"

When he hesitated she added, "Sometimes you and Ma forget that I've already learned to read."

"Hattie, as usual you ask too many questions."

Harriet smiled. Then she repeated the word her parents hated to hear, especially if she repeated it three times in a row. That word was *why*.

"Well, you see"—Lyman hesitated as he searched his mind for a diplomatic answer—"you look just like me; and I'm not very good looking. Your mother is the pretty one! That's why I married her." He rubbed his chin. "Hattie, you're a fast learner. You *are* bright. Even Judge Reeve's wife said so. If you will use that brilliant brain God gave you, and not be discouraged because of your firm Beecher nose, you'll really go far in life. I'll never forget how you listened to my sermon on Sunday morning. Your eyes never moved."

His comment about her listening to the sermon stung, for she knew that she hadn't listened to a word of it. She longed to confess the truth, but lacked the courage. Finally, she said, "Papa, I know I can't be a preacher."

"True. Still there are other things you can do." He handed her a trimmed log to put on the pile. "You can teach school like Sarah Pierce. Today her school is the most famous lady's school in all of America. You might even become a writer." He handed her another piece of firewood.

The children kept working long after Catherine had left for school. After all the firewood had been neatly piled and the cold frames leaned against the house, Beecher said, "Now, let's go swimming. Run along, change your clothes and be ready to go in half an hour."

Harriet and the others squealed with approval and disappeared immediately through the back door.

Located on a plateau in the northwest section of Connecticut, Litchfield was the fourth largest town in the state; and it was considered by many to be the loveliest town in all of New England. Harriet recalled:

"My earliest recollections of Litchfield are those of the beautiful scenery. . . . I remember standing often in the door of our house and looking over a distant horizon where Mount Tom reared its round blue head against the sky, and the Great and Little Ponds, as they were called, gleamed out amid a steel-blue sea of distant pine groves. To the west of us rose a smooth bosomed hill called Prospect Hill. I spent many a pensive, wondering hour at our playroom window watching the glory of the wonderful sunsets that used to burn themselves out amid the voluminous wreathings or castellated turrets of clouds—vaporous pageantry proper to a mountainous region.

"Litchfield sunsets were famous . . ."

Mount Tom and similar peaks intrigued the Beecher children, for they knew that when this was Indian country, the Bantam and other Connecticut tribes used them to communicate to one another by smoke signals. These signals were especially useful when settlers were attacked by the Mohawk. Mount Tom, dubbed by the Indians *Mackimoodus*, meaning "the place of noises," had the curious habit of rumbling. And sometimes its rumblings could be heard as far as Boston. Indians explained its angry scoldings by saying that it was the home of *Hobbamocko*, the originator of human calamities.

In the years to come, Harriet frequently spent hours thinking about these superstitions.

Settled in 1720, Litchfield was named after an old cathedral town in Staffordshire, England. The major difference in the name was the spelling. The Colonists added a *t* in their version. With his hunting and fishing instincts always near the surface, Lyman Beecher loved the nearby forests, streams and lakes. His gun and fishing pole and skiff were always within reach. The magnificent forests abounded with ducks, raccoons, rabbits, quail, partridges, fox, minks—and, alas, muskrats. The streams and lakes were also alive with fish: suckers, eels, catfish, trout, perch, pickerel. Pickerel weighing as much as five or six pounds sometimes stretched out on his table.

But hunter though he was, Lyman's intense love for Litchfield centered in the fact that it was a living museum of the Revolution—a museum that could inspire his children to make their lives count. Brimming with pride, he liked to lead them down the broad avenues and point to the houses where the celebrities had either lived or were still living. Waving his hand at a freshly painted house, he would say, "That's the home of Colonel Benjamin Tallmadge. He was a member of Sheldon's regiment of Horse. He guarded George Washington. He fought in the battle of Monmouth and was the leader of the guards when Major André, the spy who worked with Benedict Arnold, was hanged.

"Over there is the home of Oliver Wolcott. He signed the

Declaration of Independence. His son was the secretary of the U.S. Treasury." A favorite building was the Sheldon Tavern, less than a block from where he lived on the corner of North and Prospect. "Washington spent a night there," he said, his voice trembling with emotion.

Harriet enjoyed viewing all these famous homes; and sometimes, along with her father, she went inside. Each time she visited the home of Judge Tapping Reeve, just two blocks south of their own home, her father said, "Aaron Burr used to live here. But never mention his name in the presence of either Judge Reeve or his wife."

"Why?"

"That's a long story."

"Will you tell me when I'm older?"

"Probably."

"Why not now?"

"Because I don't want to tell you right now."

"Why?"

Instead of answering, Lyman knocked at the door.

Inside, Harriet listened in silence as her father and Judge Reeve discussed politics.

Holding Henry Ward by the hand, Harriet followed her brothers and sister to the swimming hole. While the others swam, Harriet remained on the bank with Henry.

"Why don't you come in with the rest of us?" asked Mary.

"Because I don't want to leave Henry Ward."

"He'll be all right. We'll keep our eyes on him."

"No, I'll just sit here and watch him."

"She wants to think about Pa's sermon," teased Edward.

As Harriet endured the teasing, her conscience bothered her more than ever. Yes, she had taken credit for something she did not deserve. *But what was she to do?* She did not want to disappoint her father, nor did she long to be ridiculed. While the others laughed, she struggled with her tears. Her conscience bothered her so much she had a hard time getting to sleep that night.

2
The Fourth

For over a month before the calendar would indicate that it was July 4, 1815, Harriet's excitement began to mount. She already knew that the famous date would be on Tuesday, and that the celebration this year would be extra special.

Lyman Beecher spoke more about the Fourth than any other holiday. A reason for this was that he had been born on October 12, 1775—less than nine months before the Declaration of Independence had been signed in Philadelphia. He familiarized himself with all the battles and the way God's providence had helped the Continental Army. "Sometimes," he thundered from his pulpit, "God used a storm or a fog or a missing letter. There were even occasions when He saved the life of General Washington by causing the sharpshooters to miss although he was only a few yards away."

During the middle of June, Beecher held the congregation spellbound as he related one of the dramas that took place in 1777. "Having ordered Sheldon to send him all the effective men in his regiment, George Washington waited with tense anxiety for their arrival. Four companies under Colonel Tallmadge passed through Litchfield. Since it was Sunday, they attended services here in the old meetinghouse on our village green.

"Those were perilous times, for Cornwallis was approaching the coast with a large fleet. It seemed that the Revolution would be over within a few weeks. But Pastor Judah Champion of this congregation was a man of great faith. Facing his people, he prayed:

" 'O Lord, we view with terror the approach of the enemies

of Thy holy religion. Wilt Thou send storm and tempest to toss them upon the sea, and to overwhelm them upon the mighty deep, or to scatter them to the uttermost part of the earth. . . .

" 'Should any escape Thy vengeance, collect them together again as in the hollow of Thy hand, and let Thy lightnings play upon them. We do beseech Thee, moreover, that Thou do gird up the loins of these thy servants who are going forth to fight Thy battles. Make them strong. . . .

" 'Hold before them the shield with which Thou wast wont in the old times to protect Thy chosen people. Give them swift feet that they may pursue their enemies, and swords terrible as that of Thy destroying angel that they may cleave them down.

" 'Preserve these servants of thine, Almighty God, and bring them once more to their homes and friends, if Thou canst do it consistently with Thy high purposes. If, on the other hand, Thou hast decreed that they shall die in battle, let Thy Spirit be present with them, and breathe upon them that they may go up as a sweet sacrifice into the courts of Thy temple, where are habitations prepared for them from the foundation of the world.' "

As Harriet waited impatiently for the tediously long days to pass, she tried to hurry the time by picturing the excitement she would soon be experiencing. Each moment would be unique.

Early in the day there would be a colorful parade complete with battle flags waving in the breeze. Bands would strike up with "Yankee Doodle" and other snappy marches. Then there would be a mock battle between the Redcoats and the Continental Army. Leaders were already gathering recruits.

Signing volunteers for the Continental Army was easy. But hardly anyone was willing to be a Redcoat; for, according to the usual script, the men in red were required to suffer a humiliating defeat. When approached to be a drummer boy, an acquaintance of Harriet snapped, "Not me. I don't want to be a loser!"

Thinking as well of the small fortune she and each of her brothers and sisters would receive to spend as they wished, Harriet felt chilly waves scoot down her spine. Six cents was a lot of money! Interesting ideas about how she would spend it danced before her eyes. The stalls, she knew, would be overflowing with tiny flags, ribbons, cookies, wooden swords, firecrackers, and other delights.

When the Fourth was only five days away, Harriet found it almost impossible to sleep. Visions of parades and bands kept marching through her mind. Having rolled and tossed most of the night, she barged into her father's room even before the bacon and eggs had started to sizzle. "Pa," she shouted, "it's time to get up!"

Her father did not answer.

"Get up! Get up! Get up!" she sang.

There was no response.

After raising her voice and repeating her usual song, she watched the bottom of the bed for the emergence of his big toe. When the toe did not emerge, she lifted the covers from his face. Then she heard a voice groan, "Oh, Hattie, I'm so sick. Call your mother."

"What's the matter?" asked Roxana a moment later.

"I-I don't know. I'm s-so sick."

Roxana placed her hand on his forehead. "Is there anything that I can do?"

"Nothing. My work on earth is finished. The Lord is beckoning me home. M-maybe you'd better call the children so that I can bid them farewell."

"Nonsense! You'll be all right," assured Roxana. "You just have an upset stomach. Maybe it's something you ate. I'll send for the doctor."

"No, no. Don't call a doctor. It would be a waste of money. The Lord has summoned me. I'm ready to go."

Within minutes the children had gathered around his bed. As his groans increased, their tears began to flow. The only one who remained calm was their mother; and the reason for her composure was that she had seen her husband in this situation before.

Lyman was born two months early—so tiny and frail that the midwife commented while she was washing him, "It's a pity he ain't goin' to die with his ma." His mother died of tuberculosis two days later.

Few thought the fragment of life would live. After viewing him and noticing that he could almost be placed in a German beer mug, a lean cattle buyer drawled, "He ain't hardly worth raisin', be he?"

A young mother was employed to nurse him. Unfortunately, her milk curdled in his stomach. His father, David Beecher, a blacksmith, son of and grandson of blacksmiths, placed him in the care of a thirteen-year-old by the name of Annis. She saved his life by feeding him, spoon by spoon, with milk. Patiently and diligently she worked, hovering over him like a mother hen. As he began to thrive, she added other nourishing foods. He was then raised by his uncle and aunt, the Lot Bentons, on their farm in south central Connecticut. But in spite of the fresh farm milk and vegetables, he continued to have an erratic digestive system.

While Roxana pondered what to do, Lyman's groanings increased both in volume and intensity. "I'm dying. I'm dying," he insisted. Convinced that he would soon be gone, the children began to confess their sins and implore his forgiveness.

"Pa, I want you to forgive me. I got into a fight with Edward," confessed Mary. Catherine's confession had more substance. She had played ball on Sunday night before the third star could be seen. Soon it was Harriet's turn.

Sobbing, she held her father's hand. "I-I didn't listen to your sermon at all—I-I-I—"

"Then what *were* you doing?" questioned her mother.

"I was watching a m-mouse that put his head out of a hole just beneath the pulpit."

"A mouse?" demanded her father. His voice had become almost normal.

"Yes, a mouse! Someone had been eating in the church and they-they left a few crumbs of cheese near that hole."

"Mmmm," responded Lyman ominously.

"Mmmm," repeated Roxana with even more concern.

Eyes on Harriet, her father asked, "And what did that mouse do?"

"He seemed to be listening to your sermon."

"Are you sure?" His eyes flashed with their usual brilliance.

"Yes, Papa, I'm sure. When you talked about peace, his eyes brightened; but when you talked about hell and the judgment, he backed deeper into his hole."

After a long silence, the supposedly dying preacher exploded, "That's wonderful!"

"What's so wonderful about it?" demanded Roxana. Her frown and raised voice indicated that she had begun to worry about her husband.

"It's wonderful because it proves that Paul was right. In Romans 8:22 he said, 'For we know that the whole creation groaneth and travaileth in pain together until now.' That mouse has shown us that the millennium is on the way! I'm feeling better already. Go on down to the kitchen while I get dressed."

After breakfast, Lyman Beecher wiped his mouth, summoned his dog, Trip, grabbed his gun, and went hunting. Later that evening he returned with six rabbits.

Early on Monday, the day before the Fourth, Roxana summoned Harriet to her bedroom in order to fix her hair. After she had secured a cloth around her daughter's neck, Harriet questioned. "Ma, do you believe in slavery?"

"No, of course not."

"But aren't Zillah and Rachel slaves?"

"No, they're not slaves."

"They're black."

"All black people aren't slaves. Many blacks are born free. Others buy their freedom. Rachel and Zillah are merely bound servants."

"What does that mean?"

"It means they've agreed to work for so many years, and after their time is up, they can do anything they like. As it is, they're like members of the family. They may leave next year. Many whites are bound servants. But there are those who own slaves."

"Do they own them like cows and horses?"

"Yes, they own them just as others own farm animals."

Harriet was silent as her mother fashioned the first curl by her left temple. Then she burst out, "Ma, do slave owners also own the children of their slaves?"

"They do."

"Does that mean that if somebody owned you and pa, they'd also own Henry Ward, baby Charles, and all the rest of us?"

"It does."

"That's awful."

"Of course it's awful. I wish you could have known my younger sister, Mary. She married John Hubbard, a West Indian planter whom she met in New Haven. When she got to Jamaica she found that he had fathered a large family of children by black women. Since these children were neither black nor white, they were called mulattoes. But instead of considering them his children, Mr. Hubbard thought of them as his possessions. Like a cattle rancher, he could sell them whenever he chose. Aunt Mary was so horrified she returned to Litchfield and lived with us. She died of tuberculosis two years ago. Some of her stories gave me the chills."

"Ma, do you think there will be a time when there will be no slaves?"

"I hope so. There are some states in the United States where no one can own slaves. But six of the original thirteen states and several of the new states permit slavery. The other states are free."

"Is it allowed in Connecticut?"

"It is. But only a few families practice slavery."

"Why?"

"Because as good Christians they don't believe in it."

"What will end slavery?"

"The gospel of Jesus Christ."

While her mother was fashioning her curls, Harriet noticed several new books on her shelves. Two of them were in French. One was by Antoine Laurent Lavoisier. Pointing at it, she asked, "Ma, what's that book about?"

"It's about chemistry. Lavoisier, the author, improved gunpowder and he helped develop the new French metric system. He also showed that we can neither create nor destroy—"

"What does that mean?"

"He proved that when a candle is burned, it is not destroyed; it merely changes form."

"Oh, Ma, that's not true! The wick in my candle gets black and disappears." Harriet spoke with emphasis.

Roxana chuckled. "Hattie, my dear, you're just as willful as your pa. But you are wrong. The wick is never destroyed. It merely turns into ash and gas and heat. That's what Lavoisier taught us, and he's the father of modern chemistry."

"Ma, can you read French?"

"Of course."

Harriet's eyes lit up. "Do you know everything?"

"No. I just like to learn." She placed her comb and curling apparatus on the desk. "Now you'd better rest. Tomorrow is the big day. I still have to fix both Catherine's and Mary's hair."

Pausing at the door, Harriet exclaimed, "Ma, you may not know everything, but you're the best ma in the whole world! You're also the prettiest." She then hurried to her room. Since it was impossible to rest, she went outside.

The next day Harriet woke up excited.

Holding Henry Ward by the hand, she stood with the other Litchfield Beechers at the edge of the wide avenue fronting the village green. Lined with huge elms and already-thinning buttonballs, this magnificent avenue was one of the finest in America. Since Lyman preached as many as nine times a week in any pulpit opened to him, a constant stream of visitors from other towns and counties waved at them.

Soon they heard the distant sound of drums beating. "They're coming! They're coming!" shouted Harriet as she squeezed her little brother's hand. As the band marched on, they began playing their favorite song, "Yankee Doodle." When they neared Harriet, she struggled to lift Henry Ward so he could see over the top of the children in front of them.

Numerous cannons drawn by horses followed the band, and behind the cannon marched the cannoneers, each equipped with the long wooden ramrod that had been used to load the weapon. One of the cannoneers was a woman. She held a ramrod in one hand and a pitcher in the other.

Pointing at her, Harriet turned to her Father. "Pa, look," she exclaimed, "that's a w-w-woman!"

"Yes, I know; and you'll learn more about her in the battle that will be fought. I've read the script."

Next came Colonel Benjamin Tallmadge, the speaker for the day. Dressed in a blue and buff uniform, this hero, who had guarded George Washington, fought in the Battle of Monmouth, and had escorted the spy, Major André, to the gallows, was so loved by the people that they cheered wildly as he passed by.

Marching immediately behind the colonel were the troops. Like the others in the parade, they wore three-cornered hats; and each had his powdered hair combed in a long triangle which streamed halfway to his shoulders. These queues, as they were called, ended in a ribbon bow.

Trailing behind the better dressed veterans were a number of men dressed in rags. One was even clad in a tattered blanket. Many were barefoot and several had streaks of blood painted on their legs and feet. These poor troops drew more applause than anyone else, for everyone knew that they had endured the dreadful winter of 1777 and 1778 at Valley Forge. Although 10,000 had been stationed there, each of the spectators remembered that George Washington had written: "We have this day no less than 2,873 men in camp unfit for duty because they are barefooted and otherwise naked."

As the ceremonies proceeded, no one sang "My Country,

'Tis of Thee." It had not yet been written. Nor did they sing the "Star-Spangled Banner." This anthem had been written in 1814, but it had not yet been adopted as our National Anthem. Instead, with lusty voices and a few brimming eyes, they sang:

> Let children hear the mighty deeds
> Which God performed of old;
> Which in our younger years we saw,
> And which our fathers told.

After Lyman Beecher had led in prayer, Colonel Tallmadge stood up. "Every year on the Fourth," he began, "we honor our veterans. But this year I want to honor our women. In 1776 the Continental Army not only ran short of ammunition, but we were also short of lead with which to make bullets. Then some wise people pulled down the statue of His Majesty King George III in Bowling Green and brought it here to Litchfield.

"That enormous lead statue was dumped in Governor Wolcott's apple orchard on South Street. Wondering what to do with it, two of the governor's daughters, Laura and Mary, decided to turn it into bullets. Good organizers, they persuaded many ladies to help them.

"Up at dawn, they cut the statue into sections, melted each part, and molded it into bullets. By sunset, according to Governor Wolcott's official records, they had made 42,088. Some of those Litchfield women burned their fingers and ruined their curls. But they didn't give up. Because of them, His Majesty's own statue helped to defeat his own army.

"Another lady we must honor is Mary Ludwig, the heroine of the Battle of Monmouth, a battle in which I had the honor of participating. Most of you don't remember her by that name. That is because she is remembered by the nickname the soldiers gave her, Molly Pitcher.

"Whenever they were thirsty, the men shouted, 'Molly, pitcher!' Molly would then hurry to a nearby spring and bring them a pitcher of water.

"As the battle neared the climax, Molly kept providing water for the soldiers. She had just returned from the spring with her pitcher when her husband was wounded near the cannon he was firing. Seeing him lying there, Mary handed the pitcher to a thirsty man, grabbed the ramrod, loaded the cannon, and began firing it herself.

"The next morning, after the battle was over, General Greene presented the powder-burned Molly to Washington.

The Commander in Chief was so proud he made her a sergeant on the spot. The French soldiers were also proud. They filled her chapeau with silver coins.

"Mary Ludwig's husband died of his wounds. But Pennsylvania didn't forget her. They voted her a forty-dollar-a-year pension. And she deserved it. We would have lost that battle had it not been for George Washington himself and brave people like Mary."

After a thundering ovation in which Harriet joined, Tallmadge said, "Now I'll read the Declaration of Independence as written by Thomas Jefferson."

When he had finished reading the document, Colonel Tallmadge said, "We now break for an hour to picnic. At one o'clock we'll see Molly Pitcher in action at the Battle of Monmouth."

After the Beechers had settled on the grass just behind the cannon Molly was going to fire, Harriet turned to her father. "Papa," she asked, speaking very seriously, "will there ever be a time when someone will read a paper like that which will say that all the slaves have been freed?"

"I-I don't know. If we do, such a document would have to be signed by the president."

"Would one of our presidents do that?"

"I hope so. But before an important document like that could be signed, there would have to be many little documents signed."

"Who will write those little papers?"

"I don't know. Maybe one will be written by an abolitionist."

"What's an abolitionist?"

"Harriet, you ask too many questions! Let's stop talking and start eating. Just look at those cucumbers," he chuckled. "I wish Doctor Taylor could see them."

While Harriet was eating and feeding Henry Ward, she inched as close to the cannon as her mother would allow. After what seemed forever, forty or fifty Redcoats took positions at the edge of the green. Then a smaller number of Continental soldiers formed a zig-zag line behind the cannon. As they crouched with their muskets ready, a determined man took his place behind the big gun.

Suddenly the Redcoats began to fire. The determined man responded. The cannon leaped forward with a roar. When the smoke cleared, Harriet noticed that three Redcoats had fallen. Still, King George's men continued to advance.

While guns fired and the air quivered with the yells of the soldiers, loud voices shouted, "Molly, pitcher! Molly, pitcher!"

Molly rushed from one group to another and then returned to the imaginary spring for more water. Suddenly the cannoneer groaned, "I've been hit!" As he sprawled to the ground, Molly ran to his side. "Never mind, darling," she said. "I'll take your place." Then, without a wasted motion, she poured powder into the barrel, pushed it home with her ramrod, pretended she was rolling in a cannonball, took aim, and fired. And even before the smoke was gone, she reloaded. *Whoom! Whoom!* responded the black monster as it spat fire.

Soon the Redcoats were tossing away their guns as they fled.

"Three cheers for Molly!" shouted the crowd.

As both "armies" disappeared, Harriet said, "I'm sure glad I'm a girl."

"Why?" asked Roxana.

"Because when I grow up I'll be a woman, and it was the women who won the Revolution!"

While everyone laughed, Harriet, with Henry Ward by her side, hurried over to one of the stalls to spend their six cents.

3

Sorrow

In the midst of the evening meal, Lyman Beecher announced, "Now is the time for each of you to tell me how you spent your six cents."

All but Harriet and Henry Ward had purchased candy.

"And what did you and Henry Ward buy?" asked Lyman, focusing his eyes on them.

"Henry bought a flag," replied Harriet proudly. "I'll have to call Rachel and Zillah to show what I bought."

With bright smiles dominating their black faces, the girls pointed to blue ribbon bows in their hair.

"How do you like them?" inquired Roxana.

"We love them!" exclaimed Zillah. "They make us know that we are appreciated," added Rachel.

Lyman beamed. "Henry Ward and Harriet were the best stewards. The candy is gone. But the ribbons will last."

Being the winner, Harriet proudly beamed at her other brothers and sisters.

The older children made faces at her. But they didn't say a word, for their parents looked approvingly at Harriet.

After thoughtfully cutting a square of beef and covering it with tomato sauce, Lyman said, "Brother Spence and I have arranged to exchange pulpits next Sunday. This means you'll hear an interesting sermon. Brother Spence follows the *Old Light* idea about fore-ordination. Still, he's a good man. He's just mistaken. And don't stare at his missing ear. He's very sensitive about that."

"What happened to it?" asked Catherine, her eyes sparkling with interest.

"He was a chaplain in the war. A bullet tore it off."
"Poor man. That must have really hurt."

Two days later, Harriet discovered what she thought was a sack of onions in the nursery. She tasted one. "Ummm, that's good," she said as she took another. It was a little sweet, and she decided it must be a different variety from those her father raised in his garden. Generously, she shared her find with the other children. They all dug in, enjoying the feast. What a picnic! Mary had just devoured the last one when Roxana appeared at the door.

"Look what we found!" exclaimed the little Beechers, holding up the empty sack of peelings.

Roxana's normally serene face clouded. "Oh, my dear children," she said, sadly. "What you have done makes Mama very unhappy. Those were roots of beautiful tulip flowers, not onion roots. If you had left them alone, next summer Mama would have had great big beautiful red and yellow flowers in the garden such as you never saw."

"I'm sorry, Mama," Harriet murmured.

Feeling sorry about what she had done, Harriet followed her mother to her room. Then viewing the beautiful pictures on the wall, the rug on the floor, rows of ivory miniatures, a half-knitted sweater, and a dress she was making to give to a friend on Thanksgiving, Harriet forgot about her misdeed and became captivated by her surroundings. "Mama," she said, "why do you work so hard making beautiful things?"

"Because I love the Lord and am His child. And since the Lord made the trees and the birds and the flowers and all the lovely things, I want to do the same."

"But Mama, how do you do it? Did you make that pretty carpet in the east room?"

Roxana smiled. "Yes, I'll tell you what I did. When your pa and I moved to East Hampton, no one in the entire little town had a carpet. Many of our congregation had never seen one. When your Uncle Lot sent me some money, your pa took that money and bought a bale of cotton. I spun the cotton into coarse thread and had the thread woven into a huge sail-like sheet that was as thick as my little finger.

"But that white 'carpet' didn't satisfy me. I thought it should have some color in it, so I sent to New York for some bright colors and made them into paint. After I had decided how big I wanted the carpet, I had your pa tack it down on the floor in the garret. Then I got busy.

"I painted roses and other flowers in the center and made a beautiful border around the edge. We then laid it on the parlor floor. The carpet is still beautiful, but you should have seen it!" she smiled, a faraway look in her eyes.

"One day a deacon came to visit. Your pa pointed him to the parlor and told him to go in. Hesitating at the door he exclaimed, 'I-I can't go in 'thout steppin' on't!'

" 'It was meant to be stepped on,' replied your pa.

"After the deacon had walked over it, he said 'Brother Beecher, d'ye think ye can have all that and heaven too?' "

While they were laughing, Roxana lifted Harriet onto her lap and showed her the ivory miniature she had painted of her mother. Aiming her finger at her long, straight nose and cupid lips, she said, "Hattie, you look so much like your Grandma Foote. She's a wonderful woman."

After studying the miniature, Hattie said, "I sure wish I could paint like that. How do you do it?"

"I work at it every day. Painting isn't easy. Anyone who wants to do something well must work hard at it. God has given you a good mind, Hattie. Be sure and use it." Slipping Harriet off her lap, she stood up. "And now I must get to work on my painting so run along."

At the door, little Harriet stopped and turned, "Almost every time we have family worship, Mama, you quote a favorite scripture. It begins, 'But ye are come unto mount Zion—' I don't remember the rest. Why do you say those words so much?"

"That passage goes like this, 'But ye are come unto mount Zion, and unto the city of the living God, the heavenly Jerusalem, and to an innumerable company of angels.' That verse is found in Hebrews 12:22."

"What does it mean?"

"Oh, it means many things. To me it especially means that God is alive, that there is a heavenly Jerusalem where we will go, and that that heavenly Jerusalem is filled with angels. Those words help to keep a smile on my face. But now I must get busy. Last week I bought Miss Edgeworth's new book, *Frank*. Tonight I'm going to read a part of it to you and the children. Tell them to come to my room on time."

As Sunday drew near, Harriet kept wondering how she would manage to listen to Brother Spence without staring at the place where his ear had been. Well, she would try anyway. Dressed in her Sunday best, she sat down in the boxed pew set aside for the pastor's family.

While the meetinghouse filled, Harriet began to wonder when the guest preacher would arrive. Judge Reeve and his billowy wife took their places in the pew just to her left. Then the students from his law school occupied the pews under the left balcony. A moment later they were followed by the girls from the Pierce Academy, who filled the section beneath the right balcony.

Harriet kept wondering when the one-eared preacher would arrive. Since the clock showed that it was only three minutes to the time for the services to open, she began to think perhaps the poor man had gotten lost. Forcing herself not to turn around, Harriet focused her mind on the interior of the building and the members who sat in front and on either side. This Congregational meetinghouse made an indelible impression on her mind.

In an article which became a part of her first book, she wrote: "To my childish eye, our old meetinghouse was an awe-inspiring thing. To me it seemed fashioned very nearly on the model of Noah's ark and Solomon's temple, as set forth in my Scripture Catechism—pictures which I did not doubt were authentic copies. . . .

"Its double row of windows, of which I knew the number by heart; its doors, with great wooden quirls over them; its belfry projecting out the east end; its steeple and bell—all inspired as much sense of the sublime in me as Strasbourg Cathedral itself; and the inside was not a whit less imposing.

"How magnificent, to my eye, seemed the turnip-like canopy that hung over the minister's head, hooked by a long iron rod to the wall above! And how apprehensive did I consider the question: what would become of him if it should fall? . . .

"The glory of our meetinghouse was the singers' seat, that sublime place for those who rejoiced in the mysterious art of fa-so-la-ing. There they sat in the gallery that lined three sides of the house: treble, counter, tenor, and bass—each with its appropriate leader and supporters. . . ."

Although it was time for the worship period to begin, the pulpit-chair remained empty. Suddenly the choirs were on their feet. Each did its assigned part. Then, just as they were blending together in a mighty finale, Lyman Beecher strode onto the platform and dropped down in the pulpit-chair. His face radiated the appearance of absolute determination.

Harriet stared. Nudging her mother, she whispered, "W-what happened to Brother One-Ear?"

"Shhh," cautioned her mother. "We'll soon find out."

After what seemed to Harriet an eternity, Lyman Beecher stood in the pulpit. "Brother Spence," he began, "was to preach for us this morning and I was to preach for him. But it so happened that when I was halfway to his place, we met. After we had greeted one another, he said, 'Brother Beecher, I wish to call to your attention that before the creation of the world God arranged that you were to preach in my pulpit and I in yours this Sabbath.'

"Those words twisted me the wrong way. I replied at once, 'Then I won't do it.' And so I am here this morning. My subject being 'The Providence of God.' "

Solemnly, he opened the large pulpit Bible, slipped on a pair of steel-rimmed spectacles, read his text, waited until the silence in the pews was almost unbearable, and then began. He had mastered the techniques of great oratory and spoke with the skill of a Shakespearian actor.

"If Brother Spence thinks I do not believe in Providence, he is mistaken." That first sentence was stated in such a low voice the people had to strain in order to hear. As he continued, his volume increased. "My life was shaped by God's providence, and my children's lives are being shaped by God's providence. Signs of God's providence are everywhere. That fact was dramatized in last week's Fourth of July celebrations. Had it not been for God's providence, we would still be a British Colony."

As her father gathered the audience into the palm of his hand, Harriet glanced at Colonel Tallmadge. Shoulders erect, he was listening with the intensity of a thirsty man with a cup of cool water at his lips.

"Whenever I pass the home where Ethan Allen was born," continued Lyman as he glanced at his family, "I think of Almighty God. All of us are proud that he was born in Litchfield. But he is not remembered as a pious man. When he passed away in 1789, Ezra Stiles, the president of Yale, wrote in his diary: 'Died in Vermont the profane and impious Deist, General Ethan Allen, author of the *Oracles of Reason*, a book replete with scurrilous reflexions on revelation.' President Stiles then added: '*And in hell he lifted up his eyes, being in torment.*'

"Nonetheless, this impious man provided the *human* action that allowed God's providence to take charge. On May 10, 1775, he inspired the entire Continental Army by taking Fort Ticonderoga without the loss of a single man. And what did this blasphemous man say when the British commander demanded, 'By what authority have you entered His Majesty's fort?' He answered: 'In the name of the Great Jehovah and the Continental Congress!'

"At that time," said Lyman, raising his voice, "the Continental Congress was less than a year old. Many Colonists—even loyal Colonists—had never even heard of it. But that didn't matter, for the Great Jehovah had been overseeing the affairs of men from the beginning."

As the inspired congregation held on to every spoken word, Lyman pushed his spectacles high above his forehead, lifted his head and continued.

"God's providence," he explained, "was especially demonstrated when General Washington crossed the Delaware the second time and faced the Hessians at Trenton. Those were terrible days.

"After losing nearly three thousand men at Brooklyn Heights, Harlem, Manhattan, and Fort Washington, what was left of the Continental Army under Washington's direct command fled south across New Jersey. Panic-striken, they abandoned much of their artillery. They were in such a hurry they left their soup kettles bubbling over a fire with the day's ration of soup untouched.

"As those ragged men fled, Washington spurred them on by flailing his sword in the air, and shouting, 'Run! Run! Faster!'

"For seventeen days Washington's men retreated. And during all that time the Redcoats pursed them. Well trained, the determined veterans from England were rapidly approaching even though their artillery was constantly sinking into the mud and Washington had destroyed all the bridges behind them.

"Eventually Washington and his remnant reached the Delaware just north of Trenton, but had no means to cross."

Lyman put on another pair of spectacles. "It was already December 7. If Washington couldn't get his men across the Delaware, the war would be over. Standing on the bank, the tall man from Virginia prayed for a solution. As he pondered, he thought of the Durham boats. These huge boats had been built to freight iron ore between Riegelsville and Philadelphia.

"They got a hold of the boats and soon those long, shallow transports were poled into place and the tattered army managed to cross. And just in time, too, for the last group of men were sure they had heard the Scottish bagpipes of General Howe's men.

"Comparatively safe on the west side of the river, Washington had to decide his next move. He was beset with problems and desertions. In addition, the term of duty for most of his men would be up at the end of the month."

Lyman pushed the second set of spectacles up on his head next to the first pair and put on another set. "The events of the next two weeks were crowded with almost unbelievable providential acts. We don't have time to mention all of them. But we will consider some of the most humanly apparent ones."

Surprisingly, Lyman continued to hold his congregation spellbound—even the children.

Pausing briefly, he went on. "Since Howe didn't like the weather in Trenton, and since he had a mistress in New York, he decided to return. To him, this seemed logical; for, after all, the war was practically over and he would soon be returning to England.

"Because of this thinking, the Redcoats in Trenton were replaced with Hessians under the command of Colonel Rahl—the bloodthirsty man who boasted that he had killed more rebels than anyone else."

Shuddering, Lyman shook his head.

"As Washington planned and prayed and consulted with his staff, he decided on a brave move. Against expert advice, he determined to recross the Delaware during the night of December 25 and take the Hessians by surprise. To make sure his attack would be effective, he arranged that while he crossed at McKonkey's Ferry, General Ewing with the Pennsylvania Militia would cross a mile below Trenton, and Colonel Cadawaladar would cross at Dunk's Ferry—four miles southwest of Burlington. Having crossed, each would attack Trenton from his position.

"The password that night was *victory or death*!"

Long sermons bored Harriet. But this account was so exciting she visualized everything. She saw men huddled in boats, felt sleet on her face, and watched the ice swirl by.

"Washington," emphasized the preacher, "had many reasons to be worried. Huge chunks of ice ramming into their boats had been terrifying. One boat loaded with vital cannon balls nearly sank. His already tired men didn't get to the east bank until two-thirty on the morning of December 26. This meant he could not attack under the safety of darkness. Then an even worse hazard faced them. *It had started to rain and snow at the same time*. This wet snow and rain had so dampened the priming pans on their guns that it would be impossible to fire them. Still, even though the muskets could not be fired, the charcoal boxes prepared to operate the cannon continued to glow as vigorously as when they were lit.

"As Washington advanced toward Trenton, many of his barefoot men left trails of blood. Others were so tired they marched in semi-sleep. Washington hoped that he and his army would surprise the Hessians, who would undoubtedly be drunk because of Christmas celebrations. Unfortunately the Hessians had been informed in advance about his plans! This meant that the Continental Army was marching into a trap; for, being able to fire from cover, Colonel Rahl's men would have the advantage of dry priming pans."

Beecher paused and slowly moved his eyes across the audience. As Harriet watched him she felt her heart speed.

"This could have been the end of the Continental Army," continued the preacher, raising his voice. "But at this point God's providence took hold. As Washington was advancing, a group of no more than twenty Colonists attacked the Hessians. After the Hessians drove them away, they supposed that they were the Continental Army! (Even today no one knows who they were.) Flushed with victory, the Hessians emptied more barrels of liquor.

"While they were drinking, another chapter of God's providence unfolded. Knowing what Washington was up to, a Tory went to see Colonel Rahl. When Rahl refused to see him, this British sympathizer sent him a letter by the hand of a servant. Deep in his stupor, Rahl put it in his pocket without reading it.

"But God's providence was not completed with this negligence. As Washington marched with his mud-caked, half-naked troops, a new confidence surged through him, even though at this time he did not realize that neither General Ewing nor General Cadawaladar were cooperating with him. Ewing had not crossed the Delaware. Cadawaladar, on the other hand, had crossed, but when he found it difficult to move his cannon, he retreated over the river into Pennsylvania.

"The battle began at about eight in the morning. Sleepy and drunk from their Christmas celebrations, the Hessians were completely defeated. Colonel Rahl was mortally wounded. While he was dying, and after his uniform was removed, he pointed to the letter and murmured, 'If I had read this, I would not be here.'

"Washington's victory at Trenton gave the Continental Army the boost of enthusiasm they needed. Their victory can be attributed to only one source: *The Providence of God*!"

Lyman swept his spectacles to the top of his head and put on a fourth pair. Then after a painful silence during which Harriet almost stopped breathing, he concluded: "*Each of us was made for a purpose. Our sovereign God has a task for all of the elect. I don't know what your assigned task may be. Perhaps it's to put an end to slavery. I don't know. But I do know that if we'll get busy, God's providence will come to our aid.*"

Harriet did not understand all the moves in the Battle of Trenton that her father had described. But she was caught by the idea that God has assigned a task to each individual, and she determined that she would discover what her task was as soon as possible.

Arousing from her contemplating, she took Henry Ward by the hand and headed home. The moment she stepped into the kitchen she knew something was wrong. She looked over at Zillah, who was quietly adjusting her apron.

"Miss Hattie," she said softly, "Thomas Junior is dead."

Harriet rushed outside where the furry black corpse lay in the backyard. Kneeling beside her favorite pet, she burst into tears. That very morning, he had purred and rubbed up against her. As she tenderly stroked his fur, she saw the crimson wound in his head. This little friend, who had never caught even a mouse, had been cruelly shot.

Later at the dinner table, Catherine noticed that Harriet wasn't eating. "Never mind, Hattie," she comforted, "we'll have a nice funeral for him tomorrow." Thus consoled, Harriet managed to finish her dinner.

The next morning Edward prepared a grave beneath the largest apple tree while Mary tucked the beloved pet in a shoe box their mother had provided. Following the hymns, scripture reading, sermon, and a final prayer, William H. dropped some dandelions on the closed box while he murmured:

"Earth to earth,
Ashes to ashes,
Dust to dust."

After the grave had been filled, Catherine read a poem she had written for the occasion:

"Here lies our kit,
Who had a fit
    and acted queer.
Shot with a gun,
His race is run,
    And he lies here."

Thinking about the shortness of life and the fact that all of God's creatures had an assignment, Harriet became even more concerned about the real purpose of her own life. Thomas Junior had obviously been created to protect them from rodents. That he had failed this assignment was especially apparent to her mother. And now that his life was over, he was nothing but a dead cat.

While revisiting his grave, Harriet wondered whether she had been created to be a servant like Zillah or Rachel; or, perhaps, a housewife like her mother. As young as she was, in the depth of her heart she knew that she longed to be another Mary Ludwig. But, if she couldn't be that, she decided that she would be glad to be a duplicate of one of the Wolcott girls. The way they had organized the women to transform the statue of George III into 42,088 bullets was a real challenge. Inspired by what Laura and Mary Wolcott had done, she went over to their home and envisioned the huge pile of bullets it must have made.

That night Harriet dreamed about bullets—42,088 bullets.

Days later at the conclusion of family worship, Lyman Beecher informed his family, "We may be facing difficult days ahead. Up until now the Presbyterians and the Congregationalists have been supported by taxes. But now some radicals are trying to put an end to all that. If these radicals succeed, we'll have to raise our own money.

"Judge Reeve and his wife are coming over this afternoon to discuss this problem with me. If you want to sit around and listen, it will be fine." He then turned and shook his finger at Harriet. "But please, Hattie," he said, using the tone of voice he frequently employed when he was warning about the wiles of Satan, "I don't want you to ask about either dueling or Aaron Burr."

Harriet gave an exhausting sigh, "But, why not?"

"Because it would upset the judge."

As Judge Reeve seated himself in their best chair, Harriet's eyes followed his hand as he ceremoniously laid his gold-headed cane on the floor. With long, snowy hair drooping to his shoulders, the judge radiated the appearance of another Solomon.

Although she tried not to stare when Mrs. Reeve sank into the sofa, Harriet unconsciously held her breath. This animated Mount Tom of cultured and smiling flesh was so huge it was impossible for her to walk the short distance from her home to that of the Beechers'. Invariably she came in a horse-drawn chaise.

While the judge and his wife were having tea, the conversation centered on the possible elimination of their church support from the tax rolls. "It isn't right!" Lyman grimly exclaimed. "Connecticut is a theocracy ruled by the church. And since the Congregationalists and Presbyterians are descended from the Puritans, we are God's spokesmen. It is our duty to decide the affairs of state!"

"True," agreed the judge. "But we must remember that this is a democracy." (Reeve had lost his voice, but his whisper was clear enough for him to continue teaching in the law school he had founded in 1784.[1])

"True," Lyman exploded heatedly, "but if we lose the revenue we'll be hindered in our God-assigned task." Thoughtfully he rubbed his chin, smiled and added, "When my uncle Stephen Benton refused to pay the church portion of his taxes, the sheriff sold his heifer at an auction."

After the conversation drifted to the law Judge Reeve was attempting to squeeze through the legislature which would enable married women to dispose of their property, Harriet lost interest and slipped out the back door.[2]

Early that fall while Lyman was returning from a pastoral visit, Roxana murmured, "I have a feeling that I won't be with you long." Remembering the occasion, he wrote: "I saw that she was ripe for heaven. When we reached home she was in a sort of chill."

Roxana's illness and death made an indelible impression

---

[1]This, the first law school in America, is distinguished for having graduated 101 members of Congress, 34 Chief Justices of States, 40 Judges of Higher State Courts, 28 U.S. Senators, 14 Governors of States, 6 Cabinet members, and 3 Justices of the U.S. Supreme Court.

[2]That legislation: *Law of Baron and Femme, of Parent and Child*, etc., was passed in 1816.

on Harriet. Helping her father with his autobiography, she painted this picture:

"I remember . . . when everyone said she was sick . . . when I saw the shelves of the closets crowded with delicacies which had been sent in for her, and how I used to be permitted to go once a day into her room, where she sat bolstered up in bed, taking her gruel. I have a vision of a very fair face, with a bright red spot on each cheek, and a quiet smile as she offered me a spoonful of her gruel; of our dreaming one night, we little ones, that mamma had got well. . . . Our dream was indeed a true one. She was forever well; but they told us that she was dead, and took us in to see what seemed so cold, and so unlike anything we had ever seen or known of her.

"Then came the funeral. Henry was too little to go. I remember his golden curls and little black frock as he tried to follow us, like a kitten in the sun in ignorant joy.

"I remember the mourning dresses, the tears of the older children, the walking to the burial ground, and somebody speaking at the grave. . . .

"They told us at one time that she had been laid in the ground, at another that she had gone to heaven. . . . Henry, putting these two things together, resolved to dig through the ground and go to heaven and find her. . . .

"Although mother's bodily presence disappeared from our circle, I think that her memory and example had more influence in moulding her family, in deterring from evil and exciting to good, than the living presence of many mothers. . . .

"Even our portly old black washerwoman, Candace, who came once a week to help . . . would draw us aside and, with tears in her eyes, tell us of the saintly virtues of our mother."

The words of her father at the funeral remained with Harriet and often they came back to her as she sat grieving. With a broken voice he had said, "Roxana, you are now come to Mount Zion, unto the city of the living God, the heavenly Jerusalem, and to an innumerable company of angels, to the general assembly and church of the firstborn, which are written in heaven, and to God the Judge of all, and to the spirits of just men made perfect, and to Jesus the mediator of the new covenant, and to the blood of sprinkling, that speaketh better things than the blood of Abel."

Roxana's last hours made a deep impression on her children and those who lingered at her bedside. Judge Reeve's wife considered the last moments she spent with her extremely precious and she never forgot how Roxana admonished her sons to become missionaries.

After seventeen years of marriage, and giving birth to nine children, this daughter of Eli and Roxana Foote had passed away at the age of forty-one. But her influence remained; and, across the years, flowered. Henry Ward moved his congregation to tears when he would refer to her. "She died when I was three years old that she might be an angel to me all my life. . . . No devout Catholic ever saw as much in the Virgin Mary as I have seen in my mother." And Charles Beecher indicated his deep devotion by saying: "Roxana Foote is my madonna!"

Harriet never forgot the comfort she received from the blacks. Their sympathy and understanding helped shape her life. She reminisced: "I recollect [Candace] coming to wash our clothes when the family was assembled for prayers in the next room, and I for some reason lingered in the kitchen. She drew me toward her and held me quite still until the exercises were over. Then she kissed my hand and I felt her tears drop upon it. There was something about her feeling that struck me with awe. She scarcely spoke a word, but gave me to understand that she was paying homage to my mother's memory."

Harriet Foote, Roxana's sister, had moved in with the Beechers during Roxana's illness; and now that her sister was gone, she insisted on taking Harriet back with her to Nutplains. Little Harriet was reluctant to leave Litchfield and go with her aunt. But Aunt Harriet, after whom she had been named, was a favorite; moreover, she knew that Grandma Foote had a large collection of interesting books.

Thus, with mixed feelings Harriet mounted the coach that was to take her to Nutplains, a short distance from Guilford, nearly forty miles southeast of Litchfield. As the coach bounced over the difficult roads, Harriet fought a fresh flood of tears. She had no way of knowing that God's providence was guiding her into a wonderful future.

4

New Worlds

Living in the country in a small wood farmhouse was a new and unique, experience. Both Aunt Harriet and Grandma Foote were convinced Episcopalians, and each morning and evening read prayers out of a black book, something Harriet's father would never do. Lyman Beecher believed that effective prayers were spontaneous.

"Grandma, I know that you love Papa very much," Harriet began one day. "But when you're in Litchfield you pass our meetinghouse and go to the Episcopal church. Don't you know Papa is the greatest preacher in America?"

"Your pa is a *great* speaker," she replied as she brushed her silvery hair back with her hand, "but you see, as a member of the Church of England, I believe in Apostolic Succession."

Harriet's face was puzzled. "What's *that*?"

"Apostolic Succession means that a minister must be ordained by another who, across the centuries, was ordained by one of the original apostles. Lyman Beecher is a fine man. He has lots of ability. I'm proud that he's my son-in-law. Nonetheless, he was *not* properly ordained.

"You see, Hattie, your grandfather, my husband, Eli Foote, was an attorney. But after the Revolution, he abandoned the law to become a businessman. After we had ten children, Grandpa died of yellow fever. Since we were penniless, my father, General Ward, invited me and all my children to move here to Nutplains. He then adopted all of my children with the exception of John—"

"And why didn't he adopt John?" asked Harriet.

"Because John had already been adopted by Eli's brother, Justin Foote. Justin was a New York shipper. But now let's get back to your father. While he was attending Yale in New Haven, he used to ride over on his horse. I remember those days very well. All of us liked him. Soon, he fell in love with your mother.

"Your mother was convinced that he was the greatest man that ever lived. But, they did have a problem; you see, Hattie, your mother was an Episcopalian and he was a Congregationalist. This difference in faith made it hard for them. Soon, trouble developed. I learned about it a few years after they were married.

"Your papa worried because your dear mother had *always* prayed and had *always* gone to church and had *always* considered herself a devoted Christian. He was afraid she had mistaken the *natural* goodness in her character for real salvation. So he wrote her several long letters about it. I know that because she used to share the letters with me," Grandma Foote adjusted her glasses.

"One afternoon when I heard the sound of his horse, I had a feeling that he was a troubled man. And I was right. As he dismounted I could see dark shadows in his face. That evening while he held your mother's hand, he asked an awful question."

"What was the question?" Harriet asked, almost breathlessly.

"He said to her, 'Roxana dear, would you be willing to be damned if it was for the glory of God?'

"That question shocked your mother. But, as always, she had a ready answer and said, 'Is it wickedness in me that I do not feel a willingness to be left to go in sin? When I pray for a new heart and a right spirit, must I be willing to be denied, and rejoice that my prayer is not heard? Could any real Christian rejoice if God should take away from him the mercy bestowed?'

"Lyman was stunned by her brilliant answer. When he finally came to himself, he exclaimed, 'Oh, Roxana, what a fool I've been!' He was never quite the same after that."

Little Harriet returned to her room after tea and cake. Although she remembered the gist of what her grandmother had told her, she did not quite understand the theology that was involved. The world in which she now lived in Nutplains was completely new to her. She later wrote about the long months she had spent with her grandmother and aunt.

"Aunt Harriet was no common character. A more energetic human being never undertook the education of a child. Her ideas . . . were those of a vigorous Englishwoman of the old school. . . .

"According to her views, little girls were to be taught to move very gently, to speak softly and prettily, to say, 'Yes, ma'am' and 'No, ma'am,' never to tear their clothes; they were to sew and knit at regular hours, to go to church on Sunday and make all the responses, and to come home and be catechized.

"I remember those catechizings, when she used to place my little cousin Mary and me bolt upright at her knee, while black Dinah and Harvey the bound-boy had to stand at a respectful distance behind us. For Aunt Harriet always impressed it upon her servant 'to order themselves lowly and reverently to all their betters.' That portion of the Church Catechism always pleased me, particularly when applied to *them*, as it insured their calling me 'Miss Harriet,' and treating me with a degree of consideration that I never enjoyed in the more democratic circles at home."

Two other influences at Nutplains helped shape Harriet: her uncles, George and Samuel Foote. Although George labored on the farm all day and had calloused hands, he loved a game of chess, and had a passion for knowledge. Harriet was especially drawn to him because he was never afraid to at least try to answer her questions. In the midst of a chess game in which she was losing badly, Harriet's eyes suddenly wandered. Then she said, "Uncle George, what's dueling?"

"Ah, that's a good question," he replied after making the decisive move. "Let's go to the Rees *Cyclopedia* and see what it has to say."

As he looked up the reference, Harriet had a question. "Uncle George, can you learn about anything in those books?"

"Not *anything*. But they are crammed with knowledge. Next to the Bible, an encyclopedia is my favorite reading. . . . Ah, here's the story on dueling. 'Dueling is a system in which two people who have an argument can agree to settle it by having a fight with a deadly weapon. During their fight, they must obey certain rules. If they obey the rules, the one who kills the other is not punished. Dueling goes back to ancient times. In the fifteen hundreds four thousand duelists were killed in France in eighteen years.'

"Someday this legalized system of murder will be stopped. At least it will be stopped in America. But I'm afraid it won't be stopped until another Aaron Burr affair shocks the people into action. I—"

"Tell me, Uncle George," Harriet interrupted, "why is it that when Judge Reeve visits us, Pa tells me not to mention Aaron Burr?" Her eyes brimmed with excited curiosity.

"Don't you know?" He spoke in a tone of unbelief. "Aaron Burr ran for the presidency of the United States against Thomas Jefferson. Since the electoral vote was a tie, the House of Representatives decided on the 36th ballot that Jefferson was President. Thus, according to the law of that day, Burr was the Vice-President. Burr believed he lost because of the influence of Alexander Hamilton. Later, Hamilton also kept him from being elected governor of New York. This so angered Burr he challenged Hamilton to a duel and killed him."

"But why shouldn't I mention Aaron Burr in front of Judge Reeve?"

"You don't know?"

Harriet shook her head.

"Judge Reeve, Hattie, was married to Sally Burr, Aaron Burr's sister. Aaron even lived with them."

"Oh!" exclaimed Harriet. "Now I understand."

Uncle Samuel was completely different than George. He was the captain of a square-rigged clipper and sailed to distant ports over much of the world. He was fluent in French and Spanish; and, on his return from a long voyage, he liked to bring home things that would excite comment; frankincense from Spain, the latest books from England, swords from Turkey, mats and baskets from Morocco. He also liked to relate breathless stories about his trips and to insist that there were many brilliant people in the world who were not white.

Harriet loved to visit with this uncle and as the candles burned late into the night, her horizons were pushed back again and again. Because he seemed to know more family history than anyone else, she plied him with questions, over and over again, much to his pleasure.

In addition to her uncles' influence, Harriet succumbed almost immediately to the charm of her radiant always-smiling grandmother. Mrs. Foote's influence on her granddaughter was permanent. Years later Harriet wrote: "Her mind was active and clear; her literary taste just, her reading extensive. My image of her in later years is of one always seated at a great round table covered with books, among which nestled her work basket. Among these books, the chiefest was her large Bible and prayer-book; other favorites were Lowth's *Isaiah*, which she knew almost by heart, Buchanan's *Researches in Asia*, *Bishop Heber's Life*, and Dr. Johnson's *Works*.

"We used to read much to her: first many chapters of the Bible, in which she would often interpose most graphic comments, especially in the Evangelists, where she seemed to have formed an idea of each of the apostles so distinct and dramatic that she would speak of them as acquaintances. She would always smile indulgently at Peter's remarks. 'There he is again, now; that's just like Peter. He's always so ready to put in!' She was fond of having us read Isaiah to her in Lowth's translation, of which she had read with interest all the critical notes."

Like her grandmother, Harriet also fell in love with Isaiah. Intrigued by Isaiah's vision as recorded in the sixth chapter, Harriet studied it until it became a part of her being. She read it over and over again.

The sublime imagery in those words fascinated Harriet. In her imagination she saw the whole scene.

But it was the eighth and ninth verses that moved her to the very depths. With a mixture of questioning and worship she read that part of the drama:

> Also I heard the voice of the Lord, saying, Whom shall I send, and who will go for us? Then said I, Here am I; send me. And he said, Go, and tell this people, Hear ye indeed, but understand not; and see ye indeed, but perceive not.

Bible in hand, Harriet approached her grandmother. "Grandma," she asked, "what are the first nine verses of the sixth chapter of Isaiah all about?"

Roxana Foote laid down her knitting. "Since the Lord needed a prophet to preach to His people, and since He knew that Isaiah was the person to preach to His people, and since He knew that Isaiah was the person He wanted, he sent him a vision. Those nine verses relate what Isaiah saw in that vision."

"And what did the Lord want Isaiah to do?"

"He wanted him to warn the people about many things

and to tell them about the coming of Jesus Christ."

"Did Isaiah do that?"

"He certainly did! In the fifty-third chapter and the second through the fourth verses we read:

> For he shall grow up before him as a tender plant, and as a root out of a dry ground: he hath no form nor comeliness; and when we shall see him, there is no beauty that we should desire him. He is despised and rejected of men; a man of sorrows, and acquainted with grief: and we hid as it were our faces from him; he was despised and we esteemed him not. Surely he hath borne our griefs, and carried our sorrows: yet we did esteem him stricken, smitten of God, and afflicted.

"Those words, my child, describe the coming of Jesus Christ, who came some seven hundred years later. Isaiah was one of God's chosen people."

"Grandma, does the Lord still speak to people in our time?"

"Of course. But He does not always speak to each of His children in the same way. He spoke to Moses through the burning bush. He spoke to Saul of Tarsus in a vision while he was on his way to Damascus. He sent the angel Gabriel to tell Mary that she would be the mother of Jesus."

"Does the Lord ever speak to you?"

"Many times. But never in a dramatic way. I've never had a vision."

"Do you think the Lord might speak to me?"

"Of course."

"Why?"

"Well, the Lord has many things He wants done; and each one of us was made for a purpose. Perhaps the Lord wants you to do something special for Him."

"Do you really think He does?"

"We'll have to be patient and see."

During the months Harriet was at Nutplains, Catherine kept a stream of letters moving to her grandmother and Aunt Harriet. In her notes she often referred to Hattie and how they, especially Henry Ward, missed her. Harriet was therefore not surprised one day when her father pulled in with his carriage.

"Hattie," he announced after he had lunched, "it's time for you to come home. You will soon begin going to school."

"And where will I go?" Harriet's eyes danced with excitement.

"Since Sally Pierce won't take anyone until they're twelve, I'm sending you and Henry Ward to Widow Kilbourne's school."

Lyman was ready to leave when he suddenly stopped at the door. "I've lost my hat," he said.

Harriet looked for his hat all over the living room and kitchen. Unable to find it, she said, "Papa, maybe you left it in the carriage." Skipping outside, she soon returned with the missing ministerial top piece. After putting it on his head, he remarked, "Hattie, I don't know what I'd do without you!"

5

A Churning World

Widow Kilbourne's school on West Street was only a few blocks from the Beecher home. There, on its split-log benches and with Henry Ward in tow, Harriet began her formal education.

The teacher was strict. She relied on two systems to force knowledge into the minds of her little pupils. Both were effective. "Repeat after me," she liked to say in her cracked-bell voice: "Cat is spelled C A T. How is it spelled? C A T. Altogether now. C A T." Her other method was threatening *with* and *often* applying a hickory stick.

Henry Ward rebelled at the idea of school. Feeling responsible for him, Harriet assumed the task of keeping him going. A letter indicates the progress the future Shakespeare of the pulpit made under that teacher.

> Dear Sister
>
> We are al well. Ma haz a baby. The old cow has six pigs.

Since Lyman knew that Henry would have to do better than that if he were to become a Congregational or Presbyterian preacher, he had him transferred to the nearby district school. But Harriet's favorite brother hated this one as much as he did the previous one. In later years, he wrote about those early experiences in his series of articles, *Star Papers*, published in *The Independent*:

> In the winter we were squeezed into . . . the farthest corner. We read and spelled twice a day. . . . All our little legs together . . . would fill up the corner with such a noise the

master would bring down his two-foot hickory stick on the desk with . . . a clap that sent shivers through our hearts. He would cry, 'Silence in that corner!' "

In the next school—for his father had him transferred—he learned to exercise his wit. "Now, Henry," said the teacher, "*A* is the indefinite article, you see—and must only be used with a singular noun. You can say *a man*—but you cannot say a men, can you?"

"Yes, I can. I can say amen, too," replied Henry. "Father always says it at the end of his prayers."

"Come, Henry, don't be joking. Now, decline *He*."

"Nominative *he*, possessive *his*, objective *him*," replied Henry.

"You see," emphasized the teacher, "*his* is possessive. Now you can say his book—but you cannot say him book."

"I do," scorned Henry with a huff. "Every Sunday I say hymnbook!"

Keeping Henry content was not Harriet's only concern. Within hours after her return, she discovered that her father's home was not the serene place she had remembered before she went to Nutplains. Zillah and Rachel were both gone and she missed their familiar presence. Their places had been taken by Aunt Esther, her father's half sister, and Grandma Beecher, his stepmother.

Feeling the need to help with the housework, Catherine dropped out of Miss Pierce's school. Her father, Catherine recalled, had a talent "of discovering and rejoicing over unexpected excellence in character and conduct.

"Thus stimulated, I for the first time, undertook all the labor of cutting, fitting and making all the clothing for the children as well as for myself." She also learned to cook.

The Beecher household ran with more efficiency than when Roxana was alive. But Harriet chafed under the new system. Esther and Grandma Beecher were dominated by two mottoes: "A place for everything and everything in place," and, worse yet: "Waste not, want not."

In desperation, Harriet fled to her father's study. There, in the attic, amidst the smell of curing hams of bacon, and with stacks of sermons and shelves of books nearby, she sat and watched as her father labored on sermons, articles, and correspondence. As the day went by she noticed that his zest for life was not as keen as it had once been. Knowing that she was an encouragement, she spent long hours with him in his study. One day while fingering through his books on theology, she noticed a thick volume entitled *Arabian Nights*. As she began to read, she became enchanted.

The first chapter related how Sultan Shahriyar insisted that whatever girl he married during the day should be executed the next morning. This was interesting! Soon Harriet's gray-blue eyes were leaping from one word to another. While the schedule of death-in-the-morning was being carried out, Scheherazade, daughter of the grand vizier, shocked her father by offering to marry the Sultan.

"He will kill you the next day!" exclaimed Father.

"Maybe so, but I want to marry him," insisted Scheherazade.

Sheherazade had a plan and was not worried. Her simple plan was to start telling her husband a story every day, then always stop in the most interesting place and not end it until the following morning. Then she would immediately start a fresh one even more exciting than the previous one, and again stop when she reached the highest peak of interest.

Breathlessly, Harriet began to read the young wife's stories. *Sinbad the Sailor* speeded her heart, while *Aladdin and the Wonderful Lamp* held her with such intensity she lost all sense of time.

Each story was more spellbinding than the previous one. One day as she was in the midst of an adventurous tale, she was told that Judge Reeve and his huge wife were coming over in the afternoon. Fearing that she might miss something important, Harriet put a marker in the book at the beginning of *Ali Baba and the Forty Thieves* and curled up in a corner of the living room.

Facing the judge, Lyman Beecher was extremely troubled. "This is about the most serious crisis I've ever faced," he groaned. "For years the Congregational church in Connecticut was *the* political force. We ran the state. We were supported by taxes. And now all that power is gone. Gone! And it's all gone because the Sabbath-breakers, rum-selling, tippling folks, infidels, Unitarians, and ruff-scuff got together."

"True," agreed Reeve in a throaty whisper. "Still, Lyman, they won the election! And all of our states, all twenty of them, are required by law to obey the majority."

"I know. I know. I know. But, Judge Reeve, how will we pay our bills?"

"Haven't you always preached that God would take care of His children?"

"I have."

"And haven't you told us to rely on Romans 8:28: 'And we know that all things work together for good to them that love God, to them who are the called according to his purpose'?"

"But, Judge, I'm a widower! I have eight children to clothe and feed and they have to be educated." He bowed his head in discouragement. "Things seem to be getting worse for the preachers," he murmured. He closed his eyes and shook his head.

"Lyman, God is still on His throne," replied Reeve as he took his wife's hand and helped pull her out of her chair. "God will show you what you should do. Didn't Calvin teach that God never fails?"

After the Reeves had gone, Harriet watched her father as he sat immobile in his chair. His eyes had lost their fire, and dark shadows smudged his cheeks. He appeared as if he had been forsaken by everyone. Worried, Harriet ventured, "Papa, what are you thinking about?"

Following an almost interminable silence, he replied, "I'm thinking about the Church of God!"

"Are we all going to starve to death?"

Instead of answering, one of America's greatest theologians got up, shuffled into his bedroom, and noisily closed the door.

Harriet was almost frantic. From the time she had returned from Nutplains, she had noticed how much her father had changed. No longer did she have to search under his bed for hungry lions. He had even stopped getting out his fiddle after the Sunday evening service and happily dancing a jig in his stocking feet as he sawed out a tune.

Worried, she approached her grandmother. "What's the matter with Pa?" she asked.

"All the Beechers are hypochondriacs," she divulged, nodding her head with confidence. "Lyman is just suffering with the hypos. He'll be all right in a day or two."

The next day after breakfast when Harriet crept up to her father's study she found him busy at his desk.

"Papa, what are you doing?"

"Hattie, I'm organizing some committees to raise money in the church. We've depended on taxes too long. Now we'll pay our own way! Sometimes the Lord has to teach us by closing a door. . . . The New Testament church wasn't supported by taxes. Paul said, 'Upon the first day of the week let everyone of you lay by him in store, as God hath prospered him, that there be no gatherings when I come' " (1 Cor. 16:2). He dipped his pen and filled another page with names. Then he turned to Harriet.

"One of the things I've learned," he said, speaking with more enthusiasm than Harriet had heard since her return, "is that God sometimes has to guide us with a club. Hattie, do you know why I'm a preacher and not a farmer?"

Harriet shook her head.

"As you know my mother died when I was born. Her name was Esther Lyman. She was Father's third wife. I was then raised by my uncle and aunt, the Lot Bentons. They had a hilly farm near Guilford. Because they didn't have children, they decided that I was to inherit their farm. But since I was always dreaming and thinking about books, I couldn't plow straight. One day as I was plowing, the old wooden plow jumped out of the furrow. Still, I kept going because my mind was on something else. This was too much for Uncle Lot. He said, 'Lyman Beecher, you'll never make a farmer! But since I'm your uncle I'm going to send you to Yale.' It was thus, Hattie, that I became a preacher. That experience proved to me that often our failures are far more important than our successes."

Eventually the Congregationalists were glad that Connecticut had been cut off from income tax. In his autobiography, Lyman confessed: "For several days I suffered what no tongue can tell, *for it was the best thing that ever happened to the State of Connecticut*. It cut the churches loose from dependence on state support. It threw them solely on their own resources and on God.

"They say ministers have lost their influence; the fact is, they have gained."

This crisis over, life continued on without ups or downs in the Beecher home. In a letter to Aunt Harriet Foote in Nutplains, Catherine mentioned the latest news: "Edward continues at South Farms. William is at Mr. Collins' store, but boards at home. Mary goes to Miss Pierce, and George to Miss Collins. Henry is a very good boy. . . . Charles is as fat as ever. He can speak a few words to express his wants, but does not begin to talk."

The smoothness in the home, however, did not continue. Early in the fall Lyman made a sudden announcement. "I am going to Boston. I may not get back for several weeks, so just keep busy."

There was a gleam in his eye when he stepped into his carriage. After it had disappeared, Harriet asked, "Why is Papa going to Boston?"

"I don't know," replied Catherine.

Esther shrugged.

"Maybe he's gone to get us a new ma," suggested Mary.

"You may be right," added Grandma. "My husband had five wives and David was the father of Lyman." She smiled.

With a book to finish, Harriet didn't speculate about her father's intentions. She had read *Ali Baba and the Forty Thieves* and now she continued with the next stories.

After several weeks of continuous reading, Harriet completed the final story. The unexpected solution widened her eyes.

"My master and sultan," said Scheherazade, after she had kissed the ground at his feet, "for one thousand and one days I have told you all the stories I know. May I, as a reward, humbly ask a favor?"

"Your wish is granted."

Scheherazade summoned a servant.

"Bring my children," she said.

The oldest child could already walk. The second could merely crawl. The youngest was confined to his crib. "Sir," she said "here are your sons. For their sakes grant me my life. Do not let the poor boys grow up without a mother." She then threw herself at his feet.

Overwhelmed, the sultan lifted her up. Then he said to her, "You are to reign at my side as my spouse as long as Allah grants us life."

That ending lifted Harriet's heart. The fact she appreciated most was that Sheherazade's stories had inspired the sultan to change the law that required each of his successors to have each wife killed the day after he married her.

When she was chided for wasting so much time reading fiction, Harriet replied, "Reading fiction is *not* a waste of time. The stories in the *Arabian Nights* changed the world!"

Later in the fall, Harriet was almost asleep when she heard a strange sound at the door. As an adult, she recalled: "We knew Father had gone away somewhere on a journey, and was expected home, and thus a sound of a bustle or disturbance in the house easily awoke us. We heard Father's voice in the entry, and started up, crying out as he entered our room, 'Why, here's Pa!' A cheerful voice called out from behind him, 'And here's your ma!'

"A beautiful lady, very fair, with bright blue eyes and soft auburn hair bound round with a black velvet bandeau, came into the room, smiling, eager, and happy-looking. Coming up to our beds, she kissed us and told us she loved little children and would be our mother. We wanted to get up and be dressed, but she pacified us with the promise that we would find her in the morning."

Harriet Porter was only twenty-seven when forty-two-year-old Lyman Beecher proposed to her. She came from a well-known family that had settled in Portland, Maine. Her father, Doctor Aaron Porter, was a distinguished physician. An uncle was Maine's first governor, another uncle, a state's senator, and, on two occasions, minister to Great Britain, while still another uncle was a congressman.

Hattie described her new mother with affectionate words: "She seemed to us so fair, so delicate, so elegant that we were almost afraid to go near her. . . . She was peculiarly dainty and neat in all her ways and arrangements; and I remember I used to feel breezy, and rough, and rude in her presence. We felt a little in awe of her, as if she were a strange princess rather than our own mama; but her voice was very sweet . . . and she took us up in her lap and let us play with her beautiful hands, which seemed wonderful things, as though made of pearl, and ornamented with strange rings."

Harriet Porter provided Lyman with a new enthusiasm for life. And the next year a college in Vermont added to his dignity by honoring him with a D.D.

Like many other fathers Lyman Beecher was concerned about the spiritual lives of his children. In 1819 he wrote to William H:

> I have no child prepared to die; and however cheering their prospects for time may be, how can I but weep . . . when I realize that their whole external existence is every moment liable to become an existence of unchangeable sinfulness and woe. My son, do not delay the work of preparation. . . . Time flies; sin hardens; procrastination deceives. . . . A family so numerous as ours is a broad mark for the arrows of Death. . . . To commit a child to the grave is trying, but to do it without one ray of hope concerning their future state . . . would overwhelm me beyond the power of endurance. . . . Let me not, if you should be prematurely

cut down, be called to stand in despair by your dying bed, to weep without hope over your untimely grave.

Lyman expressed this same concern to all of his children. But he always did so in a gentle and loving way. The second decade in the 1800s were convulsive years. The hated War of 1812—dubbed by many as Madison's War—had been fought. New states had entered the Union and these changes had inspired debates.

From the time of Harriet's birth until 1819, Louisiana, Indiana, Mississippi, Illinois, and Alabama had been admitted to the Union. Their admission had not created much of a stir. But immediately afterward when Maine and Missouri applied for admission, a nest of deadly hornets began to whirl. This was because eleven states permitted slavery and eleven states prohibited slavery. This division provided each group with twenty-two senators—an even balance. However, if Missouri were allowed into the Union as a slave state, the balance would be broken. Such a possibility frightened the states where slavery was prohibited.

By 1820 the debate had become acute. Many distinguished men such as Judge Reeve came to the Beecher home to discuss the matter. Sitting in a corner, Harriet, by now nine years old, listened to the discussions with intense interest. Some of the finer points were over her head. Nevertheless, she acquired a bold outline of the history of slavery in America.

The importation of slaves into the United States, she learned, had been prohibited in 1808. That was three years before she was born. Slavery at that time was on the decline. Then Eli Whitney's cotton gin, invented in 1794, became popular. This machine enabled a slave to produce fifty times more clean cotton than he had previously produced. And since cotton flourished in the South, the southern states gradually whitened with vast fields of cotton.

In less than ten years the export of cotton multiplied thirty times. Cotton production increased the demand *for* and the price *of* slaves. Harriet read that a southern newspaper had advertised a fifty-pound male slave for $500. Meaning he would be sold for ten dollars a pound! Harriet was horrified. The child would be about the same size as her little brother Charles.

The problem of allowing Missouri to enter the Union as a slave-state continued to churn. Henry Clay, speaker for the House of Representatives, pointed out that if Missouri were barred from statehood, southern senators would bar Maine from statehood. The Missouri Compromise, which he authored, restricted slavery from the territory secured in the Louisiana Purchase north of 36° 30′ latitude with the exception of Missouri.

Clay's compromise was duly passed. Maine became a free state in 1820 and Missouri would become a slave-state in 1821. After Lyman had explained all of this to Harriet with a map, he added. "This does not end the problem over slavery. Tom Jefferson has dubbed the compromise 'A firebell in the night.' And I'm afraid, Hattie, the old man is right even though a balance of senators has been maintained."

From the time Harriet had noticed that Zillah and Rachel were black and that Grandma Foote insisted that her black servants stand at a distance even during family prayers, she had thought about the injustice of slavery. But what could she, a mere girl, do about the terrible wickedness?

Although Harriet's life seemed uneventful, she brightened it by constantly curling up with a book. She was fascinated with Cotton Mather's *Magnalia Christi Americana*. Its tales of witches, Indian raids, and God's providence kept her mind active. Then one day she opened a book of Lord Byron's poetry. That book to her was like the secret door opened to Ali Baba by the Forty Thieves. It revealed huge caches of treasure. Spellbound, she read:

> Maid of Athens, ere we part,
> Give, oh give me back my heart!
> Or, since that has left my breast,
> Keep it now and take the rest.

Later, when she learned that Byron had a crippled foot, she loved his works all the more. *If such a handicap could not stop him, maybe her handicap of being a girl would not stop her!* But she was afraid her father would not approve of Lord Byron. Then, in the midst of her doubts, she found him reading from Byron just as he often read from Milton.

"Do you like him?" she asked eagerly.

"Hattie, I love him. Just listen to this." He then read from *The Destruction of Sennacherib*:

> For the Angel of Death spread his wings on the
> blast,
> And breathed in the face of the foe as he
> passed;
> And the eyes of the sleepers waxed deadly
> and chill,

And their hearts but once heaved and forever
grew still.

"That is a talented man!" he proclaimed. "Just think about what he could do if he would use that talent for the Lord. But I'm afraid, Hattie, that Lord Byron is a very ungodly man."

"Do you mind if I read him?"

"Of course not. Although he leads an ungodly life, his poetry, on the whole, is rather clean."

"Papa, do you think a girl might have enough talent to make some changes in the world?" Harriet eagerly studied his face.

"Certainly. Some of the world's most talented individuals have been women."

It seemed to Harriet that an eternity would pass before she was old enough to enroll in Sarah Pierce's school. Finally, however, she met the age and was duly seated with the other young ladies—many of them from wealthy homes and distant places.

Sarah's school was famous all over America. Not only did she teach the three R's, but she also graduated polite and dedicated scholars. She took a special pride in each of her charges and made a habit of questioning them about those things which she considered vital: Have you prayed? Have you been neat in your person? Have you spoken an indecent word? Have you combed your hair with a fine-toothed comb? Have you brushed your teeth?

John Pierce Brace taught composition and Harriet paid special attention to everything he said, because she hoped to become a poet someday. Strangely, the fact that she remained indifferent to correct spelling for the rest of her life became evident the day she enrolled. By a curious slip she was registered as Harriet F. Beecher instead of Harriet E. Beecher. Unconcerned, she made no effort to correct the error.

Harriet never achieved the honor roll even though her sister Mary was constantly listed as "Head of Papers." Like her father, she was unique. Unaffected by peer pressure, the fashions of the times meant nothing to her. She read what she wanted to read whether it was a part of her assignment or not.

When she was twelve, an occasion arose to submit an essay in competition with others, knowing that the three best essays would be publicly read to the literati in Litchfield. Her chosen subject was a difficult one: *Can the Immortality of the Soul Be Proved by the Light of Nature?*

Harriet studied, wrote, and rewrote. On the day the essays were to be read, she noticed that her father was sitting on the platform next to Mr. Brace. As she waited, someone began to read her essay. She remembered: "Father brightened and looked interested. At the close I heard him ask, 'Who wrote that composition?'

" 'Your daughter, sir,' was the response.

"It was the proudest moment of my life. There was no mistaking Father's face when he was pleased, and to have pleased him was past all juvenile triumphs."

6

The New Flower

Alexander Fisher had entered Yale at fourteen and graduated at the top of his class at eighteen. His genius glowed in many subjects. He published a book on astronomy, wrote another on Hebrew grammar, composed music, was a talented poet, and had ample finances.

His fame spread abroad to Europe.

Fisher had first become acquainted with Catherine when he read one of her poems in *The Christian Spectator*, a magazine published by her father. And, being an admirer of Lyman Beecher, he made frequent trips to Litchfield where he was always invited to stay for dinner. A relationship developed and soon the couple became engaged. Lyman was delighted about the match. But he was also concerned, for the young professor had not taken a stand for Christ.

After an up-and-down romance, which was broken and then mended, Catherine and the young professor agreed that they would be married after he spent a year touring the universities in Europe. That spring he set sail on the *Albion*.

Two months later, Lyman was attending a ministers' meeting in New Haven when he learned that the *Albion* had lost a rudder and crashed into the cliffs on the west coast of Ireland. There were only two survivors, but Professor Fisher was not one of them. Without waiting for his return to Litchfield, Lyman wrote to Catherine:

> My dear Child:
>
> On entering the city last evening, the first intelligence I met filled my heart with pain. It is all but certain that Professor Fisher is no more.

> Thus have perished our earthly hopes, plans and prospects. Thus the hopes of Yale College—and of our country and, I may say, Europe, which had begun to know His promise—are dashed. The waves of the Atlantic commissioned by heaven have buried them all.
>
> And now, my dear child, what will you do? Will you turn at length to God, and set your affections on things above, or cling to the shipwrecked hopes of earthly good? Will you send your thoughts to heaven and find peace, or to the cliffs and winds and waves of Ireland, to be afflicted, tossed with tempest and not comforted?
>
> Till I come, farewell. May God prepare you, and give me the joy of beholding life spring from death.

Having never experienced conversion, Catherine found it extremely difficult to face life. She lamented:

> If I attempt to turn the swift course of my skiff, it is only to feel how powerful is the stream that bears it along. If I dip my frail oar in the wave, it is only to see it bend to the resistless force.
>
> There is One standing on the shore who can relieve my distress, who is all powerful to save; but He regards me not. I struggle only to learn my own weakness, and supplicate only to perceive how unavailable are my cries, and to complain that He is unmindful of my distress.

Feeling Catherine's anguish, Lyman poured out his heart:

> My rod has been stretched out and my staff offered in vain. While the stream prevails and her oar bends, within her reach is My hand, mighty to save, and she refuses its aid.

Eventually Catherine received help from the writings of John Newton, converted slave trader and author of *Amazing Grace*. While she was overcoming her grief, she learned that Fisher had willed her his library and $2,000. When the books arrived in Litchfield, Lyman examined them carefully to make certain none of the volumes would be detrimental to his children. At first he hesitated about the novels of Sir Walter Scott. But after a thorough examination, he became assured that they were clean—and educational. From then on, the Beechers were addicted to Scott. Harriet especially loved *Ivanhoe*. One summer she allegedly read it through seven times.

Each year Lyman conducted work projects to get some of the special chores done. One of these consisted of preparing apples and quinces in order to make apple butter for the winter months. Since several barrels of what Harriet called "cider applesauce" were required each year, the entire family was kept busy. As the apples were peeled and cored Lyman kept everyone's mind occupied.

"Why," he would challenge as he brought out another basket of apples, "did Matthew write that two sparrows cost a farthing, while Luke wrote that five sparrows cost two farthings?"

As the problem was discussed, he prodded them with numerous questions, challenging their imagination. "Was Bookkeeper Matthew better at figures than Doctor Luke?" "Why didn't an editor make their figures agree?" "How can we believe the Bible if it is full of contradictions such as this?"

Eventually someone would conclude, "Both Luke and Matthew were right. The difference is because a merchant would throw in an *extra* sparrow for two farthings."

Pleased with this solution, Lyman would praise the one who had solved the problem and then change the subject.

In this manner the apple-bee, or work project, continued until the barrels were full and stored in the basement where the cider applesauce eventually froze and was thus preserved.

Having returned to Litchfield after visiting Alexander's family, Catherine decided that her best opportunity "to do good" was to become a teacher. Her brother Edward, who was heading the Hartford Grammar School, encouraged her. Financed by the capital she had inherited, Catherine, together with her sister Mary, opened what was described as a school "intended exclusively for those who wish to pursue the higher branches of female education."

Their institution occupied the second floor of a harness shop at the Sign of the White Horse on Main Street. It was well located, for Hartford was on the stage route between Boston and New York City. Moreover, stages frequently stopped at the nearby Ripley's Coffee House.

Neither Catherine nor Mary was adequately trained to teach the subjects they announced. But that did not deter them. Having Beecher determination, they learned quickly. After school, their candles burned late into the night while they pored over Latin, rhetoric, chemistry, logic, history, and other subjects.

The school prospered.

One day, Catherine approached Harriet and asked, "Why don't you attend our school?"

"I would love to," answered Harriet. "But how would I pay my tuition and board and room?"

Lyman Beecher solved the problem. He had made a deal with Isaac Bull, a Hartford wholesale druggist, to board his daughter Catherine so that she could attend Sarah Pierce's school in Litchfield. Now he asked if he would do the same for Harriet. Catherine also agreed to waive the tuition requirement.

Upon her arrival in Hartford, Harriet learned that she had an entire bedroom all to herself. This was a new and wonderful experience. Two classmates, Catherine Cogswell, the prettiest girl in school, the daughter of a distinguished physician and Georgiana May, who had lost her father and had a special need for companionship, became lifelong friends.

Hartford, with its population of 5,000 was, to Harriet, a huge metropolis. Window-shopping with friends was like walking down the main street of heaven. Fashion shops with their silk dresses were especially attractive. Pausing in front of one of them, Harriet pointed through the picture window. "Do you see that silk dress?" she said. "Someday I'm going to have one of them. And it's going to have a bustle."

"That's just a dream," replied Georgiana, slowly shaking her head. "Only the rich can afford silk dresses with bustles."

"Maybe so. But someday Harriet Elizabeth Beecher is going to have a custom-made silk dress complete with a bustle."

One day during an outing with Georgiana to Hartford's Park River, Harriet confided in her friend. "I have one ambition," she said, "I'm going to be a writer."

"What kind?"

"I'd really like to be a poet, especially if I could be a great one like Lord Byron. But if I can't do that, I'd be willing to become a novelist like Sir Walter Scott."

On their way home, passing a magnificent grove of trees, the girls agreed that when they were rich and famous they would build magnificent dream-houses in the midst of that grove. "And my house," boasted Harriet, "will be a large one surrounded by flowers and trees. It will have a garden and gables. There will be an enormous parlor where I can entertain famous authors and editors. I will have paintings on the walls, and shelves bulging with the latest books. All the servants will wear bright uniforms—"

Georgiana began to laugh. "Harriet, you have such an imagination; but I hope all your dreams will be fulfilled," she added as they started home.

"They will be," Harriet determined. "Just give me time!"

The fame of Lord Bryon increased every day. His books and portrait were in almost every home. Young people copied his manner of dress and went on diets in order to attain his thinness. Conversations were embellished with his lines. If an admirer began with the quote: "I know only we loved in vain; I only feel—farewell! farewell!" the reply might be: "Fools are my theme, let satire be my song."

Harriet continued to admire him; and being aware that his poem *Childe Harold's Pilgrimage* had made him famous overnight, she decided to write a drama that might duplicate his success. Pondering her chances of impressing the literary world, she decided that her poem needed at least three ingredients: a dramatic setting, a dynamic hero, and a constant description of extravagant living. At the desk in her bedroom, she outlined the source of each ingredient.

The hero would be a rich Athenian who was also an Olympic champion. The setting would be Nero's court in Rome. And her description of extravagant living would be based on the way the Caesars wasted millions of sesterces on a single feast, which sometimes ended with a serving of hummingbird tongues.

And who would be the model for the rich Athenian and victor at the Olympics? The answer was simple. Her model would be none other than Lord George Gordon Byron! Having named her poem *Cleon*, she lifted her pen and excitedly began:

> Diversion is his labor, and he works
> With hand and foot and soul both night and day:
> He throws out money with so flush a hand
> As makes e'en Nero's waste seem parsimony.

Harriet was making progress with the poem when her notebook was discovered by Catherine. After confiscating it, she stormed: "If you have so much spare time, you can begin studying Butler's *Analogy* so that you can teach it next fall."

"Yes, ma'am!" replied Harriet sarcastically.

Brokenhearted, Harriet turned to the analogy. But she continued to dream about her lame-footed hero. Then she began to learn shocking things about him. Yes, her hero, who was more proud that he had swum the Hellespont than that he had written his greatest poems, was an ungodly man. He lived with his half sister. He chewed tobacco. And it was claimed that he had staged an orgie in which he and some friends donned long, black cossocks in the manner of medieval monks, and drank wine out of polished human skulls.

Then came the shattering news that Byron had died on April 19, the day after Easter 1824. Like his father, he died at the age of thirty-six.

Harriet wept.

That summer she returned to Litchfield. One Sunday morning while sitting in her regular pew, she immediately noticed that her father was unusually moved. Even before shoving the first set of spectacles to the top of his head, he stated sadly, "Byron is dead—gone."

Shocked to attention, Harriet and the rest of the congregation waited with bated breath for his next statement.

"I'm so sorry," he continued after a few moments and gaining control of his emotions. "I did hope he would live to know Christ and to do something for Him. What an impact he might have made." Again he hesitated while he struggled with his words. Then, with a catch in his voice, he added: "If only Byron could have talked with Taylor or me, we might have helped him out of his troubles."

Several weeks later, while her father's words about Byron were still stirring within her, Harriet again turned her gray-blue eyes to the pulpit. This Sunday her father was preaching what he called a frame sermon. Instead of weaving complex arguments about some profound aspect of one of the five points of Calvinism, he ad-libbed from the overflow. His subject was: "I call you not servants, but friends."

Harriet wiped her eyes as her father spoke from his heart. An overwhelming conviction of sin settled upon her. Then she remembered the way of forgiveness as taught in the New Testament. Overwhelmed by the fact that Christ had willingly died for her, and remembering Roxana's concern for her salvation, she quietly surrendered her life to Him.

That afternoon Harriet climbed the steps to her father's study. There, with the pungent smell of hams and bacon about her, and with Mama Kitty nursing her kittens nearby, she told her father how she felt, and related the commitment she had made. As she spoke, she felt his arms tighten about her shoulders. While his tears dropped on her head, she heard him say in a broken voice, "Then a new flower has blossomed in the kingdom today."

Hearing those words, it suddenly dawned on her that she

had been freed from guilt, that she had become a joint-heir with Christ—and, best of all, that she had been created for a purpose. Tingling with anticipation, she descended the steps two at a time and went outside. She noticed that the grass was greener, the blue head of Mount Tom on the distant horizon was more glorious than it had ever been, and the sun that evening as it courted the west with its thousand colors was far more breathtaking than she had ever noticed it to be before. Yes, Harriet Elizabeth Beecher had been born again!

Sleep was impossible as she pondered how God would use her, as a girl, in His plans and purposes. Did He want her to be a teacher, a missionary, a housewife, a writer?

As she wrestled with her thoughts, her mind went back to the time she had been with Grandmother Foote in Nutplains. During those months she had been overwhelmed by Isaiah's vision in the sixth chapter of his book.

At that time she had been too young for it to be vividly clear to her. But now, as she recalled the occasion, Isaiah's words glowed with a new meaning. Slipping out of bed, she lit a candle and studied the first nine verses of that chapter. As she reread them, she became aware of the fact that Isaiah's lines were far greater than the best lines of Lord Byron. Comparing them was like comparing a mouse to a lion. Fighting tears, she read:

> In the year that kind Uzziah died I saw also the Lord sitting upon a throne, high and lifted up, and his train filled the temple.

After she had completed the passage she returned to the fifth verse. Lingering on each word, she read:

> Then said I, Woe is me! for I am undone; because I am a man of unclean lips, and I dwell in the midst of a people of unclean lips: for mine eyes have seen the King, the Lord of hosts.

After praying for understanding, she studied the following three verses, which especially impressed her.

> Then flew one of the seraphims unto me, having a live coal in his hand, which he had taken with the tongs from off the altar: and he laid it upon my mouth, and said, Lo, this hath touched thy lips; and thine iniquity is taken away, and thy sin purged. Also I heard the voice of the Lord, saying, Whom shall I send, and who will go for us? Then said I, Here *am* I; send me. And he said, Go, and tell this people, Hear ye indeed, but understand not; and see ye indeed, but perceive not.

Getting on her knees, Harriet prayed, "Lord, touch my lips with a coal from off the altar, and show me what I am to do."

As she waited, she did not receive a specific answer. Still, she felt an assurance that her prayer had been heard, and that the Lord was preparing her for a specific purpose. With new confidence, she pinched out the candle and was soon asleep.

A few years later, having recalled this occasion, Harriet wrote to her brother Edward, "He has given me talents and I will lay them at His feet, well satisfied if He will accept them. All my powers He can enlarge. He made my mind and He can teach me to cultivate and exert its faculties."

7

Darkness at High Noon

Knowing that she would be leaving for Hartford the next day, Harriet slipped over to the cemetery to where her mother, her little sister, the first Harriet, and her stepbrother Frederick were buried.

Lingering a long moment in front of Roxana's grave, Harriet pondered about her recent conversion, and how it assured her that she and her mother would be together again someday. Remembering her father's words, "Then a new flower has blossomed into the kingdom," she vowed that she would live and work in a way to honor her mother, the dearest friend she ever had.

Still sobbing, she walked over to her sister's grave. Had she lived she would be seventeen now—three years older than herself. Moved by thoughts about what her sister might have accomplished, Harriet prayed that she might "double up" and complete both her sister's assignments and her own.

Finally, she went over to the grave of Frederick—her stepmother's first child. Born in 1818, he had passed away two years later. Viewing the still-raised mound of earth, Harriet reflected on the uncertainty of life.

Since it was still late afternoon, Harriet wandered over to the fence enclosing the backyard of the Walcott home.

"May I help you?" asked Sam, the tall black gardener, walking toward her.

"Oh, no. I'm just thinking about the way the women melted George III and turned him into bullets."

Sam leaned on his hoe and chuckled. "The women did a good job," he smiled. "Those 42,088 bullets helped earn our freedom." He picked up the hoe and started to walk away. Then he stopped. "You know, Miss Hattie," he added, speaking very thoughtfully, "I wish we had some more statues we could turn into bullets."

"You mean you'd like to start another war?" Harriet frowned.

"Oh, no. I'm against war. Nevadaless, somethin' has to be done 'bout slavery. Miss Hattie, it ain't right for one man to own another. My old pappy was a white man, but I was sold as a slave."

"How could that be?" Horrified, Harriet stared.

"Because my mother was black."

"Who sold you?"

"My pappy sold me. Sold me in 'Orleans for one thousand dollars."

"Your own father sold you?" Harriet's eyes widened in disbelief.

"Yep. My own pappy sold me."

"Why?"

"Because he was in debt."

"Are you a slave now?"

"No, ma'am. I bought my freedom."

"Well now, Sam, if you had some statues to melt, what would you do with them?"

"Don't know, Miss Hattie. 'Deed I don't." Digging out a weed as he considered the problem, he continued. "But ah'll tell you what ah tinks. Ah tinks if someone could turn a chunk of history into a statue as Lot's wife was turned into salt, and den change dat statue into words, da words could change people's hearts."

"What would you do with the words?" asked Harriet, curiously.

"String 'em into stories. Mebbe a book. Miss Hattie, everyone has a tender spot inside him. Even da meanest slaveholder has a soft spot. If somebody could touch dat soft spot, he could change his ways. 'Deed, he could."

"Ah 'member when I was bein' sold down in 'Orleans. It was a summer day just like dis and da birds were singin' just like dey is singin' here now. As I was waitin' for someone to buy me, ah seed a fair-skinned woman who was holdin' a little boy by the hand. While I was watchin', da auctioneer pointed at her with his mallet.

"Speakin' through his nose, he said, 'Sasaphras is a might nice gal. Has religion. Don't steal. Sews. Has good teeth. Works hard. Cooks. Her pancakes melt in your mouth.' Den da man turned and spat a stream of terbakker juice. Next, he pointed to the ball and chain around her ankle. 'She's also good lookin'!' he added as he winked at the men who was a-crowdin' round the platform. He spat again. 'But da owner has a problem. His problem is dat he don't want to separate da mother from her son. Because of dat, we'd like to sell 'em together. Both together would make a fine buy. The young'un is a mighty fine boy. He'd look nice in a smart uniform by a front door.

" 'But if none of you gentlemen comes up with 'nuff money, ah'll be forced to sell 'em separately. Ah don't wanna do dat 'cause ah'm a kindhearted man. Deed ah am. Dat little boy needs his mammy!' Da brute hesitated. Den he said, 'Sometimes ah goes to church.'

"When he said dat, Miss Hattie, da whole crowd howled. Day 'bout split dere sides 'cause dey knew what kind of a critter he was."

He stepped closer to the fence. Mimicking the stance of the auctioneer, he pointed at Harriet and boomed in a nasal tone, "Wal, now, ladies and gentlemen, let's keep a-goin'. This good-lookin' gal and her son are bein' sold together. Do I have a bid? Five hundred dollars. Who'll make it six? Six hundred. Who'll make it seven?"

Harriet was spellbound.

"Dat's da way it went," explained Sam, shifting back into his normal voice. "When da bids stopped at twelve hundred dollars, da man decided to sell 'em separately. Ah'll never forget how Sasaphras busted up. She got on her knees. 'Please sell us together,' she begged. 'Please! Please! Please! If you'll sell us together ah'll work mah fingers to da bone. Ah'll do anything. Deed ah will.'

"But, Hattie, no one would go high 'nuff; and so she was sold to one man, while her son was sold to da other. Ah'll never forget how she screeched when dey dragged him away. While she was a-weepin', I saw dat hardhearted auctioneer turn his back to da crowd. But dis time, Miss Hattie, he didn't spit even though he had a fat wad in his cheek. No, Hattie, he didn't spit—"

"What did he do?" demanded Harriet, leaning against the fence.

"He wiped his eyes. Yes, Miss Hattie, dat's what he done. He wiped his eyes. Den he blew his nose. Words, Miss Hattie, words like bullets have power. Terrible power. Sometimes words, dramatic words, have even more power den bullets."

Deeply moved, Harriet was almost in a trance as she slowly returned home. The impromptu drama and Sam's statement about the power of words had lodged in her heart.

As the coach made its way toward Hartford, Harriet leaned back in her seat to enjoy the luxury of daydreaming. It was a lovely day. Cumulus clouds formed into patterns overhead. The countryside was green. Birds circled. Cattle and sheep grazed near the freshly painted barns. It was a day meant for dreams, and Harriet quickly became lost to hers.

It was great to be a flower in the kingdom! Better yet, it was exciting to be a *special* flower, a flower that had been planted for a special purpose. Searching her heart, she discovered that she was quite willing for God to make that decision. Still, she longed to be a poet. Oh, if she could only be another Byron—a good Byron. If she could merely approach his greatness, her greatest joy would not be that she had swum the Hellespont. Oh, no. It would be that at the age of fourteen she had accepted Christ.

Carried away, she visualized bookstores displaying her latest volume—a slender hardback with her name Harriet Elizabeth Beecher in gold letters on the spine. What would be the title of her latest, which a series of presses could not produce fast enough for an eager public? She imagined herself sitting at a desk heavy with books and hearing a buyer saying, "Miss Beecher, I have all your books; and I think *The Lord's Harp* is by far the best one. Husband says you remind him of Lord Byron. As for myself, I think you're better."

In the midst of her dream she was shaken into reality when the carriage stopped in front of an inn and she was at her destination.

After arranging her room, Harriet went over to see her father's friend, Dr. Joel Hawes, pastor of the First Congregational Church in Hartford.

"Please, sir, I want to join the church," she said.

"Mmmm. Have you ever been converted?"

Harriet related the story of her conversation and her father's words when she met with him in his study.

"Mmmm. I see." He studied her in the manner of a judge about to pronounce a death sentence. "Harriet, do you feel that if the universe should be destroyed, you would be happy with God alone?"

Harriet's heart sank. But she managed a feeble, "Y-yes, sir."

His face still grim, the pastor continued, "You realize, I trust, in some measure at least, the deceitfulness of your heart, and that in punishment for your sins God might justly leave you to make yourself miserable as you have made yourself sinful?"

The question pushed Harriet's spirits almost into her shoes, but she managed to whimper, "Yes, sir."

That answer brightened the pastor's face. "Since you are certain about your conversion, I'm glad to welcome you as a member into this congregation."

Although crushed by the interview, Harriet forced herself to smile. Secretly fighting her tears, she murmured, "I'll see you in church next Sunday."

While slowly descending the steps, the minister's words about the deceitfulness of her heart and the punishment she deserved for her sins pounded in the depths of her being. The memory of each statement was like a dagger. As she stepped onto the sidewalk, she noticed a robin tugging at a worm. Studying the drama, she wondered, "Am I no more important than a worm?"

Depressed, Harriet addressed a letter to her brother Edward, now twenty-three, who was studying for the ministry. Maybe he could help her. "My whole life is one continual struggle," she wrote. "I do nothing right. I yield to temptation almost as soon as it assails me. . . . I am beset behind and before, and my sins take away all my happiness."

She had just sealed the envelope when Georgiana knocked at the door.

Sitting on the edge of the bed, Harriet bared her soul. "The happiest moment in my life," she said, "was when Pa embraced me and assured me that I was a new flower that had blossomed into the kingdom. That idea filled me with joy and I began to think of all the fine things I could do with Christ. But now the pastor has convinced me that my heart is full of deceit." She wiped her eyes.

"Could it be, Georgiana, that my heart has deceived me about being useful in the kingdom?"

"Oh, I don't think so. You're just in a bad mood. You'll feel better tomorrow. I sometimes feel the same way. Depression is a part of life—especially for talented people."

"What do you mean?" Harriet's eyes widened.

"It takes talent to see trouble where there is no trouble.

That's the reason all the Beechers get so depressed. They're just too talented."

Harriet laughed. "What's the best way to get rid of depression?"

"Faith. Prayer. Work."

Harriet had no need to worry about having something to do. Catherine's school was growing, and she needed teachers. After discussing the matter with Catherine, it was decided she should teach. But Harriet was surprised and upset with Catherine's decision. "Next year, Harriet, I want you to teach Virgil," she said without blinking.

"Virgil!" Harriet exclaimed.

"Yes, Virgil."

"But I've never read Virgil, and my Latin isn't that good."

"That doesn't make any difference. Brush up on your Latin and study Virgil."

Harriet learned Virgil and taught him. Still, she remained discouraged. Addressing another letter to Edward, she wrote:

> I wish I could describe to you how I feel when I pray. I feel that I love God—that is, I love Christ—that I find comfort and happiness in it, and yet it is not that kind of comfort which would arise from free communication of my wants and sorrows to a friend. I sometimes wish that the Savior were visibly present in this world, that I might go to Him for a solution of some of my difficulties. . . . Do you think, my dear brother, that there is such a thing as realizing the presence and character of God, that He can supply the place of earthly friends? Do you suppose that God loves sinners before they come to Him? Some say that we ought to tell them that God hates them, that He looks on them with utter abhorrence, and that they must love Him before he will look on them?

An additional problem smote her. Almost all of the girls had a boyfriend. But no one was attracted to her. As she studied her face in the mirror, she asked herself, Was it because of her squarish face, or because of her prominent Beecher nose? Maybe it was her hair! Turning her head from side to side she studied her reflection.

Finally she rearranged her hair to fit the current style. The new coiffure made no difference. The young men continued to ignore her as if she were a symbol of the plague.

In order to get her mind off her despair she took long walks, read current books, and forced herself to laugh even amidst heartbreak. She listened closely to the pastor's sermons, went to parties, lingered on her knees, and studied the Bible.

Remembering the inspiration she had received from the sixth chapter of Isaiah, she reread the first nine verses. They were as glorious as ever. Isaiah's vision, she remained convinced, was still the most inspiring incident in the entire Old Testament. At one time she had been convinced that God would favor her with a similar vision in which He would indicate what she was supposed to do with her life. But no such vision had ever come to her—and time was passing. She was already fifteen!

Pondering why she seemed to have been ignored, she wondered if she were similar to Luke's fifth sparrow—fit for nothing but to inspire a buyer to part with an extra penny.

Harriet's feelings of uselessness remained. She felt useless when she prepared for bed. She felt useless when she read her Bible. Even her dreams impressed her with her uselessness, and when she shuffled off to school her feelings of uselessness intensified. A single question dominated her mind: "Why, oh why, was I born?"

Once in a mood of deep despair while she was sitting with Georgiana on the bank of the Park, she confessed, "I know I'm a preacher's daughter, and I hate to say it, but I almost agree with the words of Lady Macbeth."

"And what was that?"

"Don't you remember? She wailed:

> 'Out, out brief candle!
> Life's but a walking shadow, a poor player
> That struts and frets his hour upon the stage,
> And then is heard no more; it is a tale
> Told by an idiot, full of sound and fury,
> Signifying nothing.'

"I know that's pretty strong, but—"

"Oh, Harriet, don't talk like that! You're just in one of your moods."

"Maybe so, but Georgiana, do pray that God will show me what I'm to do with my life. I'm terribly afraid that my heart has deceived me. I sort of feel that I'm enduring a darkness at high noon."

But in spite of her feelings of uselessness, Harriet continued to work without pay in order that her brothers might continue studying for the ministry. Deep down inside she was convinced that none of her brothers were quite as useless as she. Moreover, she enjoyed a great satisfaction in helping them.

Following a long session with Virgil, Harriet eagerly responded to the sharp rap at the door. "Have interesting news," announced Catherine as she stepped inside. "Pa is moving to Boston."

"Boston!" exclaimed Harriet.

"Yes, Boston."

"But Boston is full of Unitarians."

"True. Nonetheless, the Hanover Congregational Church has elected him pastor. And they really want him. They're starting him out at two thousand dollars a year. That's almost three times as much as he received in Litchfield."

"But what will he do with the Unitarians?"

"Fight them of course! As you know, Pa enjoys a good fight." Catherine turned and added, "Well, I must go now. I'll see you in church on Sunday."

Since the next day was Saturday, Harriet insisted that Georgiana go with her for a long walk. Uptown, Harriet stopped at the dress shop. Pointing at a fashionable silk dress in the window, she said, "Georgiana, it won't be long until I'll walk in there and say, 'Please measure me for a dress like that, and make it wide enough at the bottom so that it will support a wide bustle.' "

"And what will you do for money?"

"Money? Money won't mean anything. Georgiana, I have a secret."

8

Boston

Harriet was nervous as she settled in the horse-drawn stage bound for Boston. The frightening story of her father's deeper-than-usual attack of hypochondria had alarmed the entire family. That story had originated in a letter William H. mailed to Edward on April 18, 1826.

In his factual and yet descriptive way, William wrote:

> I spent a week in Boston at the installation. Father was quite unwell with dyspepsia; he suffered from fear, and still does. I never knew him more cast down. He felt as though his course was finished. He had serious thoughts of sending for you, and had even written the letter, but concluded to wait and see how he got over the Sabbath. This was Friday.
>
> He took a chair, turned it down before the fire, and lay down. "Ah, William," he said, "I'm done over! I'm done over!" Mother told him he had often thought so before, and yet in two days had been nearly well again. "Yes, but I was never so low before. It's all over with me! I only want to get my mind composed in God—but it is hard to see such a door of usefulness set open and not be able to enter. . . !" I never saw him so low before.

Harriet not only worried about her father's health, but was also concerned about his continual acceptance in Boston. This cultured city, sacred to the Pilgrims, had a population of 50,000—a number so vast she found it impossible to comprehend. In addition, it was a dominion of highly intellectual people.

In contrast to this city of concentrated brilliance, Litchfield was a countrified village. Although the native had rich historic beginnings, they were still common folks and didn't object when her father preached with his boots on, climbed trees to shake down the walnuts, covered his head with spectacles, or pronounced creature *creetur*, and referred to Nicolo Paganini as *Padge-a-nigh-nigh*. But how would the Brahmans of Boston accept such crudeness? Harriet shuddered. In her imagination she visualized a leader of the church saying, "Doctor Beecher, it seems that you have forgotten that this is Boston and not Litchfield. You're just a country preacher and we're disappointed. Since we don't want to embarrass you, we'll give you the privilege of resigning next Sunday to take effect in six weeks."

The thoughts raced through Harriet's mind.

After changing horses five times, the almost one-hundred-mile journey was nearing an end. Harriet was excited that she would soon be with her parents. Finally the stage rattled into the depot and came to a stop. From the window, she spotted her father. A moment later she stepped onto the pavement and he cried, "Welcome to Boston!" Gathering her into his arms, he kissed her on both cheeks.

While leading her to his shiny new carriage, Lyman Beecher said, "Your stepmother and I are delighted that you'll be spending the summer with us."

"How are you feeling?" asked Harriet.

"Fine."

"I heard that you were pretty low when you first came."

"Indeed I was. The devil had me by the nose. But after I started preaching I felt better. My six sermons on temperance really shook them up. But the Lord has blessed us with revival and I've been baptizing and taking in members ever since. Since I'm free this afternoon, I'll take you around. Have you had your lunch?"

"No."

"Fine. Your Ma has prepared a big feed. She can't wait until you get home."

All of the Beecher children, with the exception of Henry Ward and the older ones who were in school studying for the ministry, were present when Harriet stepped into the living room. After they had greeted her, she asked them to tell their ages.

Charles, with whom she and Henry Ward had shared a room when they were small, replied a little boastfully, "I'm eleven."

"And how about you, Isabella?"

Eyes on the carpet, Isabella shyly held up four fingers.

After picking up Thomas and smoothing his hair, Harriet kissed him and inquired his age.

"He doesn't know his age," scoffed Charles. "He's only two."

(Isabella and Thomas were her father's children by Harriet Porter.)

"And where's Henry Ward?" asked Harriet after she had seated herself by the fireplace.

Lyman laughed. "Henry's afraid that his mother's prayers will be answered and he'll become a preacher," he said, rubbing his hands. "When we first came to Boston he wasted his time in school. All he really wanted to do was to go down to the wharfs and watch the ships. One day the rascal dropped a note addressed to his brother in a place where he knew I'd find it.

"The note mentioned that if he couldn't get my permission to go to sea he'd run off, that he was determined to be a seaman."

"The sea!" exclaimed Harriet. "Henry Ward going to sea? I can't believe it."

"Yes, the sea. The next day I asked Henry to help me saw wood. While we were working, I said, 'Henry, what would you like to do with your life?'

" 'Go to sea,' he replied.

" 'Do you want to be just a common sailor, or would you rather be an officer in the navy?'

" 'I want to be a midshipman and finish as a commodore,' he said.

"I then replied, 'In order to do that you must begin a course in navigation and study mathematics.'

" 'I'm ready,' he answered with great enthusiasm.

" 'Well, then,' I said, 'I'll send you to Amherst. There, you can start your preparatory studies; and if you do well, I'll try and get you an appointment at Annapolis.'

"Henry agreed to all that, and now he's enrolled at Mount Pleasant Collegiate Institute."

"How's he doing?"

"Very well. His hero is Lord Nelson. He's working hard. He's discovered the joy of learning. The boy doesn't know it, but I'll soon have him studying for the ministry! Ah, but that raises a problem. Training my boys for the ministry costs a lot of money." Shaking his head he continued. "If it weren't for yours and Catherine's generosity, I'd be sunk."

The table was crowded with dishes loaded with vegetables and meats. Harriet merely picked at her food.

"What's the matter?" asked her stepmother. "Are you ill?"

"Oh no. I guess I'm just tired," managed Harriet. "It was a long trip. We stopped to change horses five times and the roads were so rough."

"You'll probably be all right in a day or two. Next week we'll go shopping and I'll show you the new styles that are coming out."

"Are clothes expensive here?" asked Harriet, perking up.

"They're dreadfully expensive." She shook her head and stroked the side of her face. "Last week I found a black silk dress. It had covered buttons and was just what I need for weddings, and your pa has many weddings. But it was too costly. The price was higher than Henry's tuition! Lyman makes three times as much money in Boston as he did in Litchfield. Even so, we're squeezed for cash. Milk and eggs cost a fortune." After studying Harriet for a moment, she added tenderly, "Hattie, you look tired. You'd better rest."

Leading the way upstairs she paused at the top and motioned with her hand toward a door at the end of the hall. Opening the door, she pointed inside. "This is your room," she said, speaking rather proudly. "You'll be all by yourself. Now get some rest. Your father has to finish an article for his new magazine. He'll be down in an hour or two and show you around."

Wearily, Harriet hung her dress in the closet and stretched out on the bed. It seemed to her that she had barely closed her eyes when there was a tap on the door. "'I'll be ready to go in half an hour," announced her father.

As the horse clip-clopped down the street, Lyman kept pointing to items of interest. "We live on the north side," he explained. "At first your mother didn't think she'd like this side. Now she loves it. For one thing we're near Copp's Hill—"

"Copp's Hill?"

"It's a cemetery where dozens of Puritans are buried."

Moments later, he tethered the white mare at the meetinghouse and unlocked the door. Flinging his hands at the row upon row of pews, he said, "Hattie, when I first came and saw all those empty pews, a vacuum formed in my stomach. I was fearful. Since the congregation only had thirty-seven members, I wondered how we'd ever fill them." He laughed. "I need not have worried. Today, we have people in the aisles!"

He led the way up to the pulpit.

"At the last auction, choice pews brought as much as thirteen hundred dollars—people are that eager to come to church. Yes, Hattie, my dear, the good Lord wanted me here in Boston, and He's bringing many into His kingdom."

After a hurried tour around the inside of the building, he said, "Now we'll climb Copp's Hill." As the mare struggled up the cobbled street, he continued, "Boston is built on three hills: Beacon Hill, Fort Hill, and Copp's Hill. To me, Copp's Hill is the most important one—"

"Why?"

"When I first came to Boston I was so low in spirits I almost died. I loved the people in Litchfield and I wondered how I'd ever compete with all the intellectualism and wealth on Beacon Hill. Then when I was about to give up, I followed this road right to the top. Each gravestone in the cemetery spoke to me. Many Puritans are buried there; and as I moved to each marker, I thought of their lives. It seemed to me that I was treading on sacred ground."

After tethering his horse at the graveyard, he wound his way over to the grave of Cotton Mather. "Born in 1663, died in 1728," he read.

Harriet bent over the tablelike tomb resting on an oblong foundation of bricks. "I adored his *Magnalia Christi Americana*," she confessed. "That book inspired me to become a writer. He must have worked day and night. I read that his name was on four hundred and fifty publications."

"He *was* brilliant," agreed her father. "Entered Harvard at eleven and finished with honors at fifteen. Ah, but Hattie, he ruined his reputation by being so hardhearted at the Salem witch trials. No one will ever forget how they burned those poor women. The Salem trials were a blot on America." He stepped over to another marker. "Even so, Cotton Mather, God bless him, was a Congregational preacher," he sighed.

While they moved from one marker to another, Harriet became very serious. "Papa, do you remember when you told me that I was a new flower that had blossomed in the kingdom?" she asked.

"I do."

She then related the statements made by Joel Hawes.

"That was wrong, Hattie. Terribly wrong! Jesus said, 'But whosoever shall offend one of these little ones which believes in me, it were better for him that a millstone were hanged about his neck, and that he were drowned in the depth of the sea' (Matt. 18:6). Still, you must forgive him. Joel doesn't know any better. I used to be just like him. I remember when anyone told me that they were anxious about their soul, I immediately asked them about their digestion—"

"Digestion! Why?"

"Because I wanted to know if their anxiety was caused by the Holy Spirit or a stomach. Your mama and stepmother straightened me out on that. They made me understand that God is love, and that He never—never—turns anyone away."

"Pastor Hawes also told me that my heart is deceitful—"

"It is. All hearts are deceitful. That's why Cotton Mather wanted the accused women burned. But only God really knows our heart."

Harriet frowned. "But, Papa, how could such a wise man as Mather be deceived?"

"Easy. Many are deceived. They trust in their feelings rather than the Word. If our brother had gone to the Bible he would have read that Jesus taught us that we should love them and show them where they are wrong, not burn them."

"I'm still confused."

"About what?"

"I-I keep wondering whether I really did blossom into a flower and become a part of God's kingdom."

After putting his arm around her shoulders, Lyman said, "Do you not know that you cannot love and be examining your love at the same time? Some people, instead of getting evidence by running in the way of life, take a dark lantern, get down on their knees, and crawl on the boundary up and down to make sure they have crossed it. If you want to make sure, *run*, and when you come in sight of the celestial city and hear the songs of the angels, then you'll know you're across."

"In other words, you mean I shouldn't worry about it and simply get busy?"

"Of course! I keep very busy. I've started a Bible society, a Tuesday night prayer meeting, a missionary organization—and a few other things. I believe the Lord is coming soon, and we must hurry up and get ready for His coming reign." He helped Harriet get into the buggy. While they were going down the hill, he continued in a serious tone of voice. "The Puritans who are buried in Boston gave their lives for the truth. But now the Unitarians are trying to take over. They've already captured more than one hundred of our churches." He shook his head.

"The Unitarians are polished and quick-witted. They've already dominated Harvard. But they don't believe in the Trinity or the divinity of Jesus; and anyone, Hattie, who doesn't believe in the divinity of Jesus is an infidel!"

"I know, Papa, but what am I to do with my life?" Her face creased with anxiety.

"The Lord will tell you."

"How?"

"By opening or closing doors."

"Do you think I might have a vision the way Isaiah did?" She studied him carefully.

"You might. But I wouldn't count on it."

"Have you ever had a vision?"

"No."

After they arrived home and the horse had been unharnessed, Lyman suggested, "Hattie, if I were you I'd go to bed early and sleep in and relax all day. Sunday will be a busy day and I have a lot of things I must do."

Hattie had just seated herself at the table for lunch the next day when her father rushed into the room. "Had a strange experience this morning," he announced after he had tossed his hat on the floor by the door.

"Believing I'd stepped into this house, I sank into a chair near the fireplace and pondered over a sermon. As I was outlining it in my mind, I noticed a French clock on the mantlepiece. Puzzled, I said, 'Wife, where did you get that clock?'

"My question was answered by a strange voice! 'Dr. Beecher,' it said, 'I fear you've made a mistake.' Looking around, I discovered that I was peering into strange faces. Worse yet, those smiling people were Unitarians!" He laughed. "Ah, but they were very gracious. They even invited me to visit them again."

After everyone had stopped laughing, Harriet said, "Papa, you've been working too hard. Why don't you rest and then later today prepare for Sunday?"

"Rest!" he exploded. "I've no time to rest. There are three people I must visit. One is anxious about his soul. And I've a committee meeting this afternoon at four. I also have to work on my sermon." Rising up he headed for his attic study. At the foot of the steps, he paused. "Hattie, God made the Beechers in order to help change the world. Don't forget that. And if we're to change the world we have to keep busy."

Mrs. Beecher smiled. "That doesn't mean that you should

not rest, Harriet. Now, go to your room and get some sleep."

After a short nap, Harriet was awakened by the sound of voices downstairs. Wide awake, she thought about the Sunday services and all the new people she'd meet and because of this she removed her Sunday dress from the hanger and crept down the steps and into the kitchen.

"Mama," she whispered, "I must iron my dress."

Pointing at a dozen irons at the rear of the stove, her stepmother said, "They're already hot."

After testing the iron with a wet finger, Harriet asked, "Mama, are there many young people in this congregation?"

"Many. Your father really attracts young people."

"Are—are any of them studying for the ministry?"

"Of course. If Pa had his way, every young man would be a Congregational preacher," she laughed. "Why do you want to know?"

Harriet blushed. "Well, I know Papa wants all my brothers to be preachers, and so . . ." Her voiced trailed as she attacked a bit of lace.

Moments later having finished the ironing, Harriet asked, "Mama, do you think I should have a different hairdo?"

"What's wrong with the way it is?"

"Nothing. But I think that since I'll have to redo my curls anyway, you might fluff it up a wee bit."

"Why would you want to do that?"

"I'm barely five feet tall! A little fluffing would make me look taller."

"All right. Just sit down in front of the mirror and I'll see what can be done."

9

A Dog, A Petticoat, and Two Lanterns

As in Litchfield, the Beechers had family worship before breakfast. On Harriet's first Sunday in Boston, she paid special attention as her father knelt with them and prayed in the most intimate way:

"Come, Lord Jesus, here where the bones of the fathers rest, here where the crown has been torn from thy brow, come and recall thy wandering children. Behold thy flock scattered on the mountain—these sheep, what have they done? Gather them, gather them, O Good Shepherd, for their feet stumble on the dark mountains."[1]

Breakfast over, he rushed off to finish getting dressed. Harriet smiled as he bellowed, "Ma, where's my collar?" and a little later, "Ma, where are my suspenders? Ma, where's my coat?"

Fortunately, on this occasion, the long-tailed coat was located in the closet and in good condition. As he slipped into it, Harriet remembered another occasion that had become a family legend. On that never-to-be-forgotten Sunday he had located his ministerial coat without difficulty. Unfortunately he couldn't wear it. On the previous Sunday as he was rushing to the meetinghouse from an emergency, he passed the creek and noticed a fish darting close to shore. Reaching for his pole he kept tucked by a nearby tree for such opportunities, he caught it. Not knowing what to do with his prize, he slipped it into his coat pocket. Forgotten, it remained there

[1]Autobiography by Lyman Beecher, Vol. 2, p. 112. This prayer as it was remembered by Harriet Beecher Stowe.

all week. That Sunday when he slipped the coat on, the putrid smell drenched the entire room.

While the family held their breath, Roxana produced another coat that she had just repaired and deposited the other in a nearby laundry bag.

Lyman Beecher's dilemma this morning was worse than the previous near-disaster. The problem was that he hadn't prepared his sermon! In her reminiscences, published in her father's autobiography, Harriet accounts the way he composed sermons.

"The time that he spent in actual preparation was not generally long. If he was to preach in the evening he was to be seen all day talking with whosoever would talk, accessible to all, full of everybody's affairs, business, and burdens, till an hour or two before the time, when he would rush up to his study, and throwing off his coat, after a swing or two with his weights to settle the balance of his muscles, he would sit down and write quickly, making quantities of hieroglyphic notes on small, stubbed bits of paper, about as big as the palm of his hand. The church bells would begin to ring, and still he would write.

"They would toll loud and long, and his wife would say, 'He will certainly be late,' and then she would be running up and down the stairs to see that he was finished, till just as the stroke of the bell was dying away, he would emerge from the study with his coat in disarray, come down the steps like a hurricane, stand impatiently protesting while female hands, always lying in wait—adjusted his cravat and settled his coat collar. Then he'd call loudly for a pin to fasten together the stubbed little bits of sermon notes, drop them in the crown of his hat, and, hooking his wife or daughter like a satchel on his arm, would start on such a race through the streets as left neither brain nor breath till the church was gained."[2]

This morning, the single-purposed preacher snagged his wife with one arm and his daughter with the other. As he whizzed down the streets, his coattail flying, Harriet was alarmed about her hair. Totally forgetting the women he was towing, he barged through the church door, elbowed his way through the crowds searching for a seat, and puffed up the pulpit stairs.

Left to fend for themselves, Harriet and her mother

---

[2]Beecher, op. cit., p. 114.

wedged into the pastor's pew toward the center. Seconds later, a nearly bald man bent down and pled, "If you good folks will squeeze together just a wee trifle more, I will have a seat." The people complied and with a sigh of relief he sank into the remaining space at the end of the pew next to Harriet.

"Thank you very much," whispered the grateful man. "I'm terribly tired and I was afraid that I'd have to stand." Smiling at Harriet and studying her through his steel-rimmed spectacles, he added confidentially, "I'm William Lloyd Garrison. And I suppose you're—"

The tired man's speech was interrupted by the organ.

Harriet was fascinated with her father's sermon. According to custom, he laid a solid biblical foundation and carefully buttressed it with strong, logical reasoning. Then, after pushing his spectacles high on his forehead, he outlined what the scripture meant, and what it did not mean. This accomplished, he announced numerous formidable objections to his thesis, all of which he demolished with two or three skillful blows.

As this old formula was proceeding, Harriet noticed that Garrison was taking notes. Watching out of the corner of her eye, she noticed the intensity of his lean face, thin triangular nose, straight mouth, firm, smoothly shaved chin.

Now that her father was sporting his fourth set of lenses, Harriet knew that he was about to press his arguments home—and plead for commitment. So far, he had done well; and Garrison's interest had remained. *But would this continue?* She knew that when her father drew in his nets, he was sometimes so carried away, he often fell into his old habit of mispronouncing words and even using faulty grammar. Silently she prayed that he would not make any embarrassing slips this time.

But even as she was frantically directing petitions to the heavenly Father, he leaned forward, and while shaking his finger, stormed, "We must never forget *Padge-a-nigh-nigh*. That slender *Eyetalian* is one of God's choice *creeturs*. God put in his *natur'* the passion to play a violin."

Embarrassed, Harriet lowered her head, closed her eyes and sighed.

"*Padge-a-nigh-nigh*," continued her father, "had just started to play when the A string broke. Ignoring this, he continued on without hesitation. Then the E string snapped. The audience groaned. Many had waited for months, paid good money, and stood in line in the rain in order to hear the one and only *Padge-a-nigh-nigh.* Now their money was wasted! But ignoring his loss, the maestro kept playing. And his improvisation was so sublime many were pulled to the edges of their seats.

"Ah, but that wasn't the end of his troubles; for just as he was climaxing an aria, the D string parted. This meant that all he had left was the slender G string. Did he give up? Never! Stepping forward, he poured his soul into his playing. Soon, scores were wiping their eyes. Why? Because *Padge-a-nigh-nigh* could squeeze three octaves out of a G string and it seemed to them that they were listening to a choir of angels.

"In spite of the other strings, that single G string—that lonely G string—was faithful.

"Many of us are like a violin. Some have broken strings. Others have strings that are out of tune. Those problems don't really matter. What really matters is for us to be fully yielded to Jesus Christ, the truly great musician. *Padge-a-nigh-nigh* is charming Europe by rubbing a few strands from a horse's tail over the insides of a cat. But we—you and I—are God's masterpiece; and we are joint-heirs with His only begotten Son."

After the service, Garrison beamed at Harriet. "Dr. Beecher is truly a great preacher." He shook his head. "By mispronouncing Paganini's name he made his illustration stick. It was like adding a barb to an arrowhead. What a man! What a man!"

Harriet stared, swallowed, shifted her feet, and finally murmured, "Dr. Beecher is my father. He's very unique." Then turning she accompanied her mother out of the sanctuary.

After the noon meal Harriet rose and went up to her father's study. "Pa," she said, "excuse me. I don't want to disturb you. But, do you know a man named William Lloyd Garrison?"

"Oh, he's a very zealous young man. A printer, I believe. Someone mentioned he's looking for work. I like the fire in his eyes. Someday he'll stir the world."

"Pa, I loved your sermon. That wonderful story about Paganini stirred me. But—" she bowed her head and her eyes became shiny. "But I'm afraid that there isn't even a broken string in my life—"

"Nonsense. As I've told you before, God made you for a purpose."

"But what is it?" A note of desperation edged her voice.

"I don't know."

"When will God tell me?"

"Give Him time."

"But, Papa, last June 14 I was fifteen and now I'm going on sixteen! I'm getting old. If the good Lord would tell me what He wants me to do, I could start preparing so that I could do it more effectively." She wiped her eyes and blew her nose.

"How do you know that He's not preparing you now?"

"In what way?"

"I really don't know. But God didn't call Moses until he was eighty, and yet He arranged for him to be prepared across many years in Pharaoh's court. Hattie, God works in mysterious ways." He smiled and then changed the conversation. "I understand that Ma is taking you sightseeing tomorrow. She really knows the city and I'm sure you'll have a good time."

Having tethered the horse in Dock Square, Harriet's mother said, "It was in this area, just a few blocks from our church, that the Revolutionary War started. The trouble began on March 5, 1770. There had just been a heavy snow. The streets were white. Snow had always been a temptation to some of the young people, for the British red-coats were excellent targets. And that night they were especially zealous because a lobsterback had been quoted as saying, 'Them in Boston as would eat their suppers Monday night would never eat another.' And remember, Hattie, this was Monday night!

"About eight o'clock four young men were sauntering down the street when they came upon a hot-tempered Irish sentinel armed with a club. After telling him he shouldn't be armed at that time of night, they tried to pass him without answering his challenge. This started a fight.

"One of the men was knocked down and another had his clothes torn and his arm slightly wounded. Soon a group of soldiers poured out of their barracks. Since they were not supposed to have guns, they were armed with shovels.

"As the confusion increased, church bells began to ring; and since church bells often signalled a fire, hundreds poured into the streets carrying leather buckets filled with water. While the half-dressed crowds milled around, more arguments erupted. Eventually a group of redcoats armed with guns appeared.

"Frightened, Henry Knox pushed through the crowd to the side of Captain Preston. 'Take your men back,' he warned. 'If you don't there'll be bloodshed and you'll be held responsible.'

" 'I'm sensible to that,' the captain agreed.

"Then Crispus Attucks, a giant mulatto slave who bought and sold cattle for his master, began to wrestle with a soldier over a musket. While they wrestled, the shouting increased. Finally someone cried, 'Fire!' Attucks was the first one killed. Altogether, five Americans died. Others were wounded.

"That, Hattie, was the flame that started the Revolution. Since it's close by, let's walk over to the home of Paul Revere. It's just a little way up the street."

"Wasn't Paul a bell-ringer at the Old North Church?"

"Yes, he was. He began ringing them when he was fifteen. Later, when he became a silversmith, he made their silver chalice, which is still used to this day when they serve communion."

"Then Paul Revere was a Congregationalist?"

"Of course. The Old North Church used to be called Christ's Church. Some even call it Mather's Church. That's because four generations of Mathers preached there. Your father told me that he took you up on Copp's Hill where Increase and Cotton Mather are buried. Both of them preached at Old North Church and were great men."

After viewing the Revere home, Harriet and her mother walked over to the famous church on Salem Street. As they were walking, Mrs. Beecher continued. "It's important to know why that old meetinghouse is so important in the story of the Revolution. This is what happened:

"The news that General Thomas Gage had assigned 700 men to seize the ammunition and cannon stored at Concord had leaked out. (Some think his American wife couldn't keep the secret.) But no one knew whether the raid would be by land or by sea. Thus it was arranged for Paul Revere to have lanterns hung high in the steeple of Old North Church. One lantern would warn that the British were coming by land. Two would warn that they were coming by sea."

When Harriet and her mother reached the church, they found a guide showing a group of tourists around the interior of the building. Pointing to pew number 62, the stout man said, "That is where General Gage and his wife used to sit." Then, aiming his finger at the organ loft, the colored windows and numerous marble busts, he related an interesting story about each item. "The communion plate," he explained, "was presented by King George II." Next, after leading the group to the base of the high pulpit, he added, "His Majesty also presented the congregation with the *Vinegar Bible—*"

" 'Vinegar Bible!' " exclaimed Harriet. "What's that?"

"It was called the Vinegar Bible because in the 1719 printing, the word vineyard in the Gospel of Luke was printed vinegar. But, as it turned out, his gift was a prophetic one; for, due to the lanterns in the steeple, this church became vinegar to His Majesty's grandson, George III!" He laughed. "Come to the steps leading to the steeple and I'll show you what I mean."

Opening the door and waving his hand upward, the guide continued, "Contrary to popular belief, Paul Revere did not hang the lanterns in the steeple on the 18th of April, 1775. Instead, they were placed there by Robert Newman, an outspoken Son of Liberty and known to the British. Newman risked his life by lighting and hanging them there.

"Since it was known that the British intended to arrest Samuel Adams and John Hancock, Paul Revere agreed to dash over to Lexington and warn them. To save time, he asked young Newman to hang the lanterns for him.

"Newman agreed without hesitation.

"Robert was in a very dangerous position, for he lived with his mother in North Square. Their home was just a short distance from the church. In addition, a number of British officers had been billeted with his mother. How was he to perform his task at such a tense moment without raising suspicion? He went to bed early. Then, while the officers in the living room below were laughing over their cards, he slipped out the window and dropped to the ground.

"John Pulling, a vestryman from the church armed with the key, was waiting for him. Together they went to the church. Pulling unlocked the door, relocked it after Newman entered, and stood guard.

"Having climbed the steeple before, Newman knew just how to proceed. From the closet he selected two lanterns and slowly eased his way up through the darkness to the bells. There he rested. Then he continued higher and higher until he reached the top window. From this vantage point he could see the shoulder of Copp's Hill, the outline of Charleston where he knew eager men were awaiting his signal, and the dark hulk of the battleship Somerset which had been anchored in the Charles River to keep an eye on anyone who crossed.

"He then lit both lanterns and allowed them to shine briefly. He had to be careful. He knew that Paul Revere had, or would be, crossing the Charles in order to get to Lexington and warn Adams and Hancock to go into hiding. He didn't want to alert anyone on the Somerset."

"Were the lights seen?" asked a lady at the end of the pew.

"Yes, ma'am, they were seen. And because they were seen, the men at Concord were prepared. Without Newman's lanterns the Revolution might have ended right then. And if it had ended that day all of us would be subjects of Silly Billy, better known as George IV!"

"And we'd all be paying a tax on tea," added Harriet.

Everyone laughed.

"Now I'll tell you about Paul Revere and his famous ride," continued the guide. He wiped his face with a fresh handkerchief. "But since his ride was not in this church, it might be more comfortable if all of you were seated on this front pew."

Standing before them, the man continued. "After Revere was assured that Newman would light the lanterns, he put on his heavy boots, kissed his wife goodbye and crept into the street. The entire area that night was heavily patrolled. Ignoring the British soldiers, Revere headed to the house where his friend Thomas Richardson lived. While he was hurrying through the alleys, he discovered that his dog was following him.

" 'Go home!' he ordered. "But instead of going home, the brown spaniel faithfully remained. Finally, he got to Richardson's house; and there both Richardson and Joshua Bentley, the boatbuilder, were waiting for him just as it had been arranged.

"According to their agreement, these men would row him across the Charles where he would mount the horse John Larkin had agreed to furnish and start on his ride. The trio had reached the corner of North and North Centre Streets when Revere stopped. 'I-I forgot to bring some cloth to muffle the oars,' he said.

" 'That's all right,' whispered one of the men. 'My girlfriend lives upstairs in that house.' He made a secret whistle and when she opened the window, he told her what he needed. She tossed them her petticoat. (Years later, Revere told his children that it was still warm.) The men were about to head for the hidden boat when Revere stopped again. His problem this time was that he had forgotten his spurs! Ah, but he had a solution.

"He wrote a note to his wife, attached it to his dog's collar and sent him home. That brown spaniel headed home like a streak of lightning. And when the dog returned the spurs were attached to his collar.

"After the oars had been muffled, Revere's boat took off. They rowed by the Somerset without being detected. The horse was ready and Revere was on his way. There were two roads from Charleston to Lexington, Revere took the road that led by the gibbet—"

"What was that?" asked Harriet.

"Twenty years before, a slave who had tried to escape was executed, placed in an iron cage, and left hanging in his chains at that place. When Revere got there, only his bones were left. . . . That grim reminder indicated to Revere what would happen to him if he were caught! Instead of discouraging him, it encouraged him to ride faster. But let me read to you what happened in Revere's own words." Taking a worn book out of his pocket, he read:

" 'The moon shone bright. I had almost got over Charleston Common toward Cambridge when I saw two Officers on Horseback, standing under the shade of a tree, in a narrow part of the road. I was near enough to see their Holsters & cockades. One of them started his horse toward me and the other up the road, as I supposed to head me should I escape the first. I turned my horse short about, and rid upon a full gallop for Mistick Road.'[3]

"He continued going as fast as his borrowed horse would gallop and soon crossed the plank bridge that led into Medford. Revere later wrote: 'I awaked the Captain of the minutemen, and after that I alarmed every house till I got to Lexington.'[4]

"In Lexington, Revere went to the Clark parsonage and warned Adams and Hancock that the British were after them. He left the parsonage at one o'clock in the morning. As he continued on his horse, he kept spreading the news. 'The British are marching! Get the warning round!' Just as he was leaving Lexington, he was joined by Samuel Prescott, a young doctor from Concord who had been courting a young lady in Lexington. Here, in the book, Revere tells us what happened:

" 'When we got about halfway from Lexington to Concord,

---

[3]Beecher, op. cit. Revere's own punctuation and spelling.
[4]Ibid.

the other two [he had been joined by Dawes] stopped at a House. . . . I kept along. When I got about 200 yards ahead of them, I saw two officers under a tree. . . . The Doctor jumped his horse over a stone wall and got to Concord. I observed a wood at a small distance and made for that intending when I gained that to jump my Horse & run afoot, just as I reached it out started six officers siesed my bridel, put their pistols to my Breast, ordered me to dismount, which I did. One of them who appeared to have command there, and much of a Gentleman, asked where I came from; I told him.'[5]

"Afraid to return to Boston because of the now-aroused citizens, and not knowing what to do with Paul Revere, the British kept his horse and released him. Eventually he got back to his home."

"Did our men in Concord save the ammunition?" asked Harriet.

"Most of it. And it was saved because of Revere and Newman and their friends." The guide then turned and walked away, signaling that his lecture had ended.

As Harriet mounted the buggy, her mother said, "And now we'll go to a clothing store. I know you want to see some of the new fashions."

"Ma," replied Harriet eagerly, "I'm certainly glad you took me to the Old North Church. That's an experience I'll never forget! Both Paul Revere and Robert Newman must have been wonderful men."

"They were."

"Do you think God called them to do what they did?"

"I don't know. God is sovereign. If it hadn't been for them we might not have our freedom."

"I think God must have arranged their lives for a special purpose," Harriet said firmly. "And just think, some unimportant things became extremely useful. If it hadn't been for a petticoat the oars would not have been muffled and the men on the Saratoga might have discovered them. And if it hadn't been for the dog, Revere would not have had his spurs; and without his spurs he could not have made his ride. And if the vestryman had not had the key and opened the door, Newman could not have signaled with his lanterns. And if—"

"Hattie," interrupted her mother, "we've reached the dress

---

[5]Ibid.

shop, and this is the finest in all of Boston. The best dressed women all shop here."

Stepping inside, Harriet was amazed at the many rows of dresses, racks laden with enormous hats, tables overflowing with gloves for all occasions, and still more racks loaded with blouses. "Do you have silk dresses?" asked her mother.

"Certainly. Just step this way," replied the smiling, middle-aged lady dressed in a green blouse topped with a snug, star-shaped white collar. Pointing to a stunning black dress, complete with a wide bustle, she said, "This is the latest." Responding to a bell, she added, "Now excuse me. A lady is being fitted for a dress. I'll be back in a moment. Just look around."

After taking the black dress off the rack, Mrs. Beecher held it up close to Harriet. "You'd look like a queen in this," she announced.

Her mind still on the Revolution, Harriet merely glanced at it and said, "Mama, did you notice that the first person killed in the Revolution was a black man? And did you notice that Paul Revere was guided on his ride by the bones of a slave hanging in an iron cage?"

"I did. But I thought you were interested in the latest fashions. Don't you like these dresses?"

"Yes, I do. But, Mama, I've been thinking that it is about time for some man to climb up a high steeple and tell the world about American slavery. Ma, slavery is a dreadful sin. It's worse than leprosy. No human being has the right to own another human being. All of us, black and white, were made in the image of God." Her voice became intense as she began to pace back and forth.

"Did you know that while we're in this shop thinking about dresses, slave families are being separated on the auction block? Slavers think nothing of tearing a child from the arms of its mother for a few dollars. Those greedy men are more concerned with money than with lives." She blew her nose. "Ma, you should have heard the stories Sam told me. Those stories would freeze your blood. Sometimes I dream about them. And did you know—?"

She was interrupted by the clerk. "Have you found anything you really like? Our sale closes today."

"They're all beautiful. But . . . Well, maybe we'd better return some other time. My daughter seems to have something else on her mind—"

"I can assure you that we have the best and the cheapest—"

"Yes, I know. Your dresses are lovely. But Hattie is more concerned with slavery right now than with fashions."

"Slavery!" balked the lady. "Slavery?" She stared and walked away.

"Yes, slavery," replied Mrs. Beecher, lifting her voice. Looking quizzically at the retreating clerk, she turned to Hattie and led the way outside.

As they were clip-clopping home, Harriet turned toward her mother. "You know, Ma, if I were a man I'd do something about slavery," she said.

"What would you do?"

"I don't know. But I'd do something!"

10

Trapped!

After a breakfast of ham and eggs, Harriet spent extra minutes before a mirror. She fluffed her hair a little higher, made certain her cuff-like collar was snug at her throat; then tightening her belt, she adjusted her curls with pins to frame her face to the best advantage—and again wiped her shoes for the fifth or sixth time.

Although trapped in the body of a girl, it might be that she could use her few feminine charms to influence a talented man to make his life count. Perhaps the Lord could use her in the same way He had used Deborah. . . .

As she and her mother waited for her father to appear with his sermon notes, the church bell began to sound. "Where's Pa?" asked Harriet.

"He's late. He mislaid a commentary. But he'll be here soon. Don't worry."

Boom! Boom! Boom! the bell tolled.

Nervously, Mrs. Beecher went to the staircase. Hands cupped to her mouth, she shouted, "Lyman! We'll be late! Hurry!"

Her only answer was the mocking sound of the bell. *Boom! Boom! Boom!*

"Hattie, you'd better go upstairs and hurry him," ordered her mother.

Harriet bounded up the steps two at a time. As she barged into the study, her father stood up. "I'm ready," he announced. "I just need a pin to bind my notes."

"Ma'll have one," assured Harriet. "We must hurry."

Halfway down the steps, the booms began to slacken.

"We'll be late," moaned Harriet.

The final boom drifted through the window just as they reached the living room.

"Your tie is crooked," wailed Mrs. Beecher. She had just straightened it when she noticed that he had a brown sock on one foot and a blue one on the other. "Dear me," she cried, "you can't go into the pulpit dressed like that! Harriet, get a pin for his notes while I rush upstairs and get another pair of socks; and while I'm doing that, Lyman, take off your shoes."

Unable to find a pin, Harriet removed the one that held a curl in place above her left ear.

One of the black socks her mother produced had a huge hole in the big toe area. "I'll have to go upstairs again," she groaned.

"Oh, no. I'll wear 'em just as they are. The shoe will cover the hole. Besides, my big toe needs some ventilation. It's a hot day."

While the preacher sat on the sofa, Harriet laced one shoe while her mother laced the other. Finally, Mrs. Beecher said, "I guess we're ready. Let's run."

"Oh, but I need my hat," objected Lyman as he rushed around the room with such speed his coattail flew upward. Both Harriet and her mother helped him search. A few seconds later, Harriet exclaimed, "There it is!" She jabbed a finger at the crosspiece under the dining room table. Sinking to her knees, she fished it out.

Lyman dropped the notes in his hat, slapped it on his head, grabbed his wife and daughter, and headed down the street toward the church like a constable rushing a pair of criminals to jail.

With a sigh of relief, Harriet sank into the pew next to her mother. As she relaxed, she wondered if she had smudged her dress when she knelt down. A quick glance indicated that it was all right. Then she thought about the curl above her left ear. Her fingers indicated that it was out of place. While the congregation was standing during the second hymn, she nudged her mother. "I need an extra pin for my curl," she whispered.

"I'm sorry I don't have an extra one," she replied.

"What will I do?"

"Don't worry. It looks all right."

Harriet swept her eyes over the congregation. When she failed to see Garrison she felt better. Nonetheless, she was a little tense. What would people think?

Lyman Beecher's sermon was aimed at the Unitarians. "The newspapers denounce me," he said. "I find that quite encouraging, for whenever I hit the mark the feathers fly. Of course, I have to be careful. Years ago, I threw a book at a skunk and I've learned from experience . . ."

This morning he spoke louder than usual, pounded the pulpit in the manner of a blacksmith, and waved his hands and arms as if he were fighting a cloud of attacking hornets. Spellbound, Harriet moistened her lips. Thoroughly intrigued, she forgot all about the wayward curl until she saw her reflection in the mirror at home.

In the midst of family dinner, Lyman complained, "I wasn't at my best this morning."

"Oh, I thought you did very well," replied Mrs. Beecher. "I've never seen you so animated."

"Humph! Animated? Yes, I was animated." He continued to eat for a while, then said, "Remember: The emptier the wagon, the louder it rattles."

Everyone laughed and Harriet reached for the mashed potatoes.

The next Sunday the meetinghouse was crammed to standing room only. Harriet's curls were in place and her dress was impeccable. But Garrison was not present; nor did he show up the next Sunday nor the next. After he had missed seven Sundays, Harriet approached her father.

"Garrison is a very vigorous young man," replied Lyman. "I also have missed him. I've heard he's been visiting various churches. Let's pray that he doesn't get mixed up with the Unitarians!"

Harriet's "vacation" in Boston soon came to an end and she returned to Hartford. "I don't know what I'd do without you," Catherine confessed as her younger sister stepped off the stage. "We've been having a revival. Many have been converted, and I'm planning a new building. All of us will have to keep our candles burning."

Catherine, Harriet discovered, had an increasing assurance that her calling in life was to promote "female" education. Energized by this absolute confidence, her older sister made use of every second of the day; and she saw to it that her teachers did the same. She never asked anyone to do what she was unwilling to do. Nonetheless, her actions made it apparent that she considered any candle that was not burning simultaneously on both ends an unworthy candle.

Harriet not only taught classes, but was also enrolled. In her book, *True Remedy for the Wrongs of Women*, Catherine described a typical day for her teachers as they taught in the crowded basement room, which was all she could afford in the beginning:

> Upon entering the school they commenced . . . the business of keeping order. . . . To this distracting employment was added the labor of hearing a succession of classes at the rate of one every eight, ten, or fifteen minutes. . . .
>
> By the time the duties of the day were over, the care of governing, the vexations of irregularities and mischief, and the sickness of heart occasioned by feeling that nothing was done well were sufficient to exhaust the animal strength and spirits, and nothing more could be attempted till the next day rose to witness the same round of duties.

Each night when Harriet prepared for bed she was utterly exhausted. In addition she faced the heart-rending fact that she was not able to ascertain what God wanted her to do with her life. Again and again she prayed, "Dear Lord, I long to do Thy will. Please show me what I'm to do with my life. More than anything, I want to be obedient to Thy will."

But even though she always felt a calm assurance after each session of prayer, she never received any clear-cut direction. Her frustrations continued to deepen. Often, in despair she wished she'd never been born. Sometimes for days she couldn't get to sleep until midnight. After one horrible night of rolling and tossing, she barged into her father's study.

"Papa," she wailed, "I wish the Lord would show me what I'm to do with my life. I'm utterly confused. Catherine has received her assignment and so has Henry Ward, Edward, William H. and Mama. But even though I pray by the hour and search the Bible, I don't receive a hint—not even a hint—as to what God wants me to do." She broke down and wept. "Pa, I'm trapped. Yes, I'm trapped!"

Lyman smiled. Putting an arm around her shoulder, he said, "God loves you. He planted you in His kingdom for a purpose. Flowers take time to grow. And sometimes, as you've noticed, a tree bears more fruit after it's been injured." He pulled her close.

"Do you mean God allows me to be frustrated for a purpose?"

"I don't know. God allowed the Jews to work as slaves in

Egypt; and He allowed them to be exiled in Babylon. He also allowed me to be orphaned when I was born, and for you to lose your mother."

Harriet silently wept for a long moment. Then she asked, "Papa, when the Lord does give me an assignment—if He ever does!—will I be successful?"

"Of course you'll be successful. But you'll only be successful in His way. Isaiah taught us that God's ways are not our ways."

Harriet dabbed at her eyes again and blew her nose. "It's terrible to be unwanted," she groaned. "It's like being in hell."

Lyman removed his spectacles. After moistening them with his breath, he carefully polished each lense. Chin cupped in his hand, he said, "Hattie, God has a plan for you, just as He has a plan for each of my children. Like you, Henry Ward was frustrated. He wanted to go to sea. But now that he's been converted, he has felt God's definite call to the ministry. I'm certain that you're being prepared for something." Putting on his spectacles he continued:

"Both my father and grandfather were blacksmiths. They were experts in fitting horseshoes and beating iron into all sorts of useful shapes. But before they reached for their hammers, they always heated the iron until it was red, and, sometimes, even white hot. I know, for I used to crank the bellows for them."

"Do you mean the Lord allows me to be in such confusion for a reason?" Harriet cried.

"I don't know. He allowed Catherine's fiancé to be drowned; and now Catherine is being acclaimed as a pioneer in female education. Someday books will be written about Catherine. I'm mighty proud of her." He took off his glasses, twirled them around with his fingers, and then put them on again. "It may be, Hattie, that God wants you to be a writer. You have a way with words, and you have a strong memory. If you were a writer, how would you describe a frustrated person if you had never been frustrated?"

Harriet sighed. "I still wish the Lord would speak to me as clearly as He spoke to Isaiah."

Lyman chuckled. "Do you remember when you were a little girl how you and some of the others ate the roots of some of your mother's flowers?"

"We thought they were onions!"

"And what did your mother say?"

"*That* I'll never forget even if I live to be one hundred. She said, 'My dear children, what you have done makes mama very unhappy. Those were roots of beautiful flowers, not onion roots.' "

Lyman Beecher opened his Bible. "Now listen to what Jesus said, 'Except a corn of wheat fall into the ground and die, it abideth alone: but if it die, it bringeth forth much fruit' (John 12:24). Do you believe that?"

"Yes, of course. But it seems to me that I'm like a grain of wheat that fell into the ground upside down."

They both laughed. Becoming serious, Harriet then asked, choosing her words carefully, "Papa, do you think that if God calls a person to a certain task, and he faithfully performs it, he will succeed?"

"Of course." He studied her suspiciously.

"Do you remember when you preached a sermon against dueling?"

"I do. And that sermon was printed and forty thousand copies of it were distributed."

"Yes, I've read it. It was a great sermon. But, Papa, listen to this: Last year when Andrew Jackson was campaigning to be president, his opponent published a pamphlet against him. It was titled 'The Indiscretions of Andrew Jackson.' I read that as well, and it stated that between the age of 23 and 60 he had been engaged in fourteen duels. He even killed a man in a duel. Let me quote what it said: 'This hero of New Orleans has been envolved in 103 hostile encounters as a participant, second, or a member of the dueling party.'[1] And now this man is our president!"

Lyman Beecher chuckled. "Hattie, you've done your research. But you are forgetting one thing. When God assigns a task to a person, that person should respond. But God is sovereign. He never tells us the precise date His assignment will be fulfilled. I have learned that He will fulfill His will when He decides to fulfill His will. Remember, Paul wrote, 'I have planted, Apollos watered; but God gave the increase' (1 Cor. 3:6). God prepared me and inspired me to preach that sermon; and God will put an end to dueling when He decides to put an end to dueling. And He will also end slavery when it is His will to end slavery."

"If that is so, why should we seek to accomplish anything?"

"Because God wants us to obey Him; and, Hattie, the hap-

---

[1]*North American Duels*, p. 190

piest people are those who respond to His commands. Our works and His will must go together. James, the half brother of Jesus, wrote: 'For as the body without the spirit is dead, so faith without works is dead also' (James 2:26). Luther didn't like that passage, and it is not a favorite with Old Light Calvinists. Nevertheless, it's true! Now Hattie, I must get to work on completing my pamphlet, *A Plea for the West.*"

Dipping his goose-quill into the ink, he began to write.

Harriet's gloom continued to haunt her. And her feeling of discouragement darkened when she considered the great success her brother Edward was enjoying. He had been the valedictorian of his class at Yale in 1822, attended seminary, was acclaimed as an athlete, and was called to the pastorate of the Park Street Church in Boston when he was only twenty-three. She had a deep affection for her distinguished brother. He had helped solve some of her spiritual problems. She frequently went to hear him at the Park Street Church; and sometimes after the service she would slip over to the nearby Old Granary Burying Ground and pay her respects to Paul Revere, Samuel Adams, the victims of the Boston Massacre, and others who were buried there.

Harriet was proud of Edward. But when she thought of his accomplishments and compared them with her own, she felt very unworthy. In the depths of one of her days of acute hypochondria, she wrote to Catherine and described the despair that had gripped her:

> I don't know as I am fit for anything, and I have thought that I could wish to die young, and let the remembrance of me and my faults perish in the grave, rather than live, as I fear I do, a trouble to everyone. You don't know how perfectly wretched I often feel: so useless, so weak, so destitute of all energy. Mama often tells me that I am a strange, inconsistent being. Sometimes I cannot sleep, and have groaned and cried till midnight, while in the daytime I've tried to appear cheerful, and succeeded so well that papa reproved me for laughing too much. I was so absent sometimes that I made strange mistakes, and then they all laughed at me, and I laughed, too, though I felt I should go distracted. I wrote rules; made out a regular system for dividing my time; but my feelings vary so much that it is almost impossible for me to be regular.[2]

Harriet's despair continued to torment her. Then her father inadvertently altered the trend of her thoughts by relat-

---

[2]*Life and Letters of Harriet Beecher Stowe*, p. 63.

ing an experience he had just had. "William Lloyd Garrison came to see me this morning," he said.

"He did?" Harriet's eyes widened.

"Yes. When he first came to Boston he got a job on the *National Philanthropist.* At first he merely set the type. Then he began to write editorials. He's full of energy. Soon, he began to fight liquor tooth and nail. I still remember one of his poems:

> What is the cause of every ill?
> That does with pain the body fill?
> It is the oft repeated gill
> Of Whiskey. . . .

"That poem was all right, and he did a lot of good fighting the traffic. But now Benjamin Lundy has given him a new cause to fight. He's persuaded him to become an abolitionist!" Lyman scowled.

"Why did he come to see you?" Harriet leaned forward.

"Because he wants me to support abolition."

"And what did you tell him?" Harriet spoke anxiously.

"I told him I had too many irons in the fire. That annoyed him. His eyes burning behind those steel-rimmed spectacles of his, he replied, 'You'd better let all your irons burn rather than to neglect your duty to the slave.'

"I didn't appreciate that. But I do admire his energy. And so I replied, 'Your zeal is commendable, but you are misguided.' Garrison didn't like that very well. He left in a huff."

"How do you think we should stop slavery?"

"We can stop it only by changing people's hearts. And we can change their hearts only by helping them to see that it is wrong. Do you remember how the auctioneer in the story Sam told you wept when he saw the boy torn from his mother's arms. It might be—" He paused in deep thought. "It might be that if someone could dramatize the evils of slavery they might—just might—shake slavers up until they'd be willing to free their slaves. Slavery, Hattie, is the worst problem we are now facing."

"Couldn't a law be passed that would stop it?"

"A law?" her father stared. "No, a law would never do any good. Not a bit of good. It would be easy to get one on the books. But no one would obey it. In 1728 when the British were in Boston, the butchers were annoyed by packs of dogs that bothered them when they slaughtered animals—often in the streets. Those dogs became very skillful in running off with their meat. The result? They passed a law that no one could have a dog more than ten inches high. Did anyone obey it? Of course not. Even Sam Adams had a Newfoundland. He named it Queque. Whenever the monster saw a redcoat, it took after him. He reached for his pen. "I think the real solution to slavery is to send all the present slaves back to Africa."

Deep in thought, Harriet returned to her room. Letting her Bible fall open to any place, it automatically opened to the sixth chapter of Isaiah. There she reread, perhaps for the one hundredth time, the last line of the eighth verse: "Then said I, Here am I; send me." Oh, how she wished she could utter those same words in response to a definite assignment! Pondering over them, she climbed the steps to her father's study.

"Hattie," he said, as he dipped his quill, "I'm absolutely rushed. I can't put off the printer another minute. He's already screaming. I have only about ten more sentences to write."

Harriet watched as his pen skimmed over the paper. As he wrote he mumbled to himself. Again and again he dipped into the ink. Then he crossed out a line, rewrote it, and stacked his papers together. "Well, that's that," he said triumphantly. He dumped the pile in his hat, mistakenly put on another hat, and hurried down the steps.

After he had disappeared, Harriet suddenly noticed that his manuscript was in his other hat, the one he generally wore to church on Sunday. Staring at it, she made up her mind in a fraction of a second. Tucking the hat under her arm, she rushed down the steps.

11

The Lure of the West

Lyman Beecher was searching frantically for his manuscript when Harriet burst into the printing office. "Papa, you put on the wrong hat!" she exclaimed, handing it to him.

Her father grabbed it, fished out the manuscript, and passed it on to the printer. Pulling Harriet close, he declared, "Hattie, you're absolutely indispensable!"

"I'm glad I have *some* talent," she laughed, leading the way down the steps. Once on the street she asked. "Papa, why are you so excited about the West?"

Quickening his pace, he confessed, "The West has everything. Rivers. Fertile soil. Trees. Game. Fish. It's a place of new beginnings. It's a place for pioneers. You know, your uncle, Sam Foote, has been all over the world. He has plenty of money. He can live anywhere he wants to live. And where has he chosen to spend his last years? Cincinnati—the gateway to both the South and Western Territories. And now, Uncle John has joined him.

"The East has been ruined by Unitarians and Catholics. The West is fresh new country. It's like New England was when the Pilgrim Fathers first arrived. If we can get the true gospel planted there, it will spread and save America. Thanks to the Missouri Compromise of Henry Clay, the Western Territories are still free from the curse of slavery."

After striding along in silence for another block, Lyman spoke again, "Hattie, I'm going to let you in on a secret. Some of the leaders at Park Street are unhappy with Edward. They say he's too much like me!" He laughed. "The truth is they don't like our New Light ideas. That door seems to be closing to him. But a much bigger one is opening." Stopping in front of a vacant lot, and glancing about to make certain no one could overhear, he lowered his voice and continued in an extremely confidential manner, "A group of seven Yale students has covenanted to spend their lives in spreading the gospel and education in the West. Their first project is to found a college in Jacksonville, Illinois. They've already secured a large building.

"When they approached Dr. Day [president of Yale Theological Seminary] for his candid advice in securing a president, he suggested your brother Edward."

"Do you think he'll accept?" asked Harriet a little amazed.

"Of course. But that isn't all. Rumors keep coming my way that a wealthy man in New York wants to sponsor a seminary in Cincinnati. And, not only are they going ahead with their plans, they have already secured the land, and they want me to be the first president."

"Are you going to accept their offer?"

"If the terms are right, and the way is clear, and if it's the Lord's will, I'll seriously consider such a call if I receive it in black and white. In the meantime we must pray that the heavenly Father will have His way."

"Do you hope that it will be His will for you to go?" pressed Harriet a little mischievously.

"Well, yes I do." He picked up a stick that had fallen across the sidewalk and tossed it to one side. "Some of the promoters are calling Cincinnati the Athens of the West. If I go, I hope most of the children will go with me. A Beecher invasion of the West could do a lot of good. I'd like to preach some New Light ideas on a new Mars Hill."

"Do you mean you feel like Abraham when he received his call to move to the Promised Land?" teased Harriet.

"In a way, I do."

They both laughed.

During the following summer weeks as Harriet noticed the eagerness with which her father studied the mail, she also prayed for directions. "Oh, Lord," she pleaded every night, "show me how I can make my life useful."

On September 14, 1830, a Tuesday she would never forget, Harriet noticed an article in the *Advertizer* about *Old Ironsides*. Intrigued, she rushed up to her father's study. "Just listen to this, Papa," she said. Standing in the doorway, and holding the newspaper to the light, she read:

> It has been affirmed on good authority that the Secretary of the Navy has recommended to the Board Navy Commissioners to dispose of the frigate Constitution. Since it has been understood that such a step was in contemplation we have heard but one opinion expressed, and that in decided approbation of the measure. Such a national pride as Old Ironsides is should never by any act of our government cease to belong to the Navy. . . . In England it was lately determined by the Admiralty to cut the Victory, a one-hundred gun ship (which it will be recollected bore the flag of Lord Nelson at the battle of Trafalgar), down to seventy-four, but so loud were the lamentations of the people upon the proposed measure that the intention was abandoned. We confidently anticipate that the Secretary of the Navy will in like manner consult the general wish in regard to the Constitution, and either let her remain in ordinary or rebuild her whenever the public service may require. (The news item was credited to the *New York Journal of Commerce.*)

Lyman Beecher laid down his goose-quill and stared. "That is just terrible," he said. "I once saw the Constitution in dock and I was so impressed I wept. Old Ironsides is a monument to American gallantry. She got that name in Madison's War (the War of 1812). During a battle with the British ship *Guerriére*, a cannonball struck her side and fell into the sea. Stunned by what he had seen, a seaman shouted, 'Huzza, her sides are made of iron.' "

Thoroughly excited, Lyman got up and paced back and forth. "If the Secretary does away with Old Ironsides," he exploded, "it will be like ripping a star out of Old Glory!"

During the rest of the day whenever Harriet met her father, he had an additional comment about the tragedy of losing Old Ironsides. At lunch, he said, "Old Ironsides showed her stamina in our war with Tripoly. Had it not been for her and her gallant men that war would have dragged on for a long time."

At supper, he added, "Old Ironsides didn't fail us. Her sails were shredded by cannon fire; her decks were reddened by heroes' blood. But now we're failing Old Ironsides! Something must be done about this tragedy. But what, I don't know." He pounded the table with such a thump the knives and forks jumped.

The next day Harriet grabbed the *Advertizer* the moment it arrived. As she studied it, her eyes caught fire. Rushing upstairs she confronted her father. "Listen to this," she all but shouted, "someone else is also disturbed about the fate of Old Ironsides." With a quivering voice, she read:

> Ay, tear her tattered ensign down!
> Long has it waved on high,
> And many an eye has danced to see
> That banner in the sky;
> Beneath it rung the battle shout,
> And burst the cannon's roar;—
> The meteor of the ocean air
> Shall sweep the clouds no more.
>
> Her deck, once red with heroe's blood,
> Where knelt the vanquished foe,
> When winds were hurrying o'er the flood,
> And waves were white below,
> No more shall feel the victor's tread,
> Or know the conquered knee,—
> The harpies of the shore shall pluck
> The eagle of the sea!
>
> Oh, better that her shattered hulk
> Should sink beneath the wave;
> Her thunders shook the mighty deep,
> And there should be her grave;
> Nail to the mast her holy flag,
> Set every threadbare sail,
> And give her to the god of storms,
> The lightning and the gale!

After wiping his eyes and blowing his nose, her father asked, "And who wrote that?"

"I don't know. It's simply signed 'H'."

"Ah, then I know who it is. It's Oliver Wendell Holmes! His father, Dr. Abiel Holmes, and I were good friends. He was a staunch Congregational preacher and we often exchanged pulpits. But Oliver Wendell has become a Unitarian." He sighed. "Even so, he wrote a stirring poem. I hope some other newspapers copy it, and it saves Old Ironsides. But I doubt that it will. Old Ironsides, I'm afraid, is doomed."

Unable to forget the stirring lines, Harriet began to investigate the circumstances under which it was written. To her amazement, she learned that after reading about the proposed fate of Old Ironsides, Oliver Wendell Holmes had been so stirred he had dashed off the poem while standing by a window. She also learned that he had just turned twenty-one and was less than two years older than she.

But Harriet didn't have time to lament that she was merely an accomplished hat-finder, while this young medical student was already a successful poet. She had to pack her things and once again head back to Hartford.

"A couple of weeks ago I had a most interesting visitor," said Catherine one day over a cup of tea. "His name is James G. Birney, from Huntsville, Alabama. He was born in Danville, Kentucky, and is quite wealthy. And—"

"What did he want?" interrupted Harriet, wondering if her sister was on the verge of a new romance.

Catherine thoughtfully stirred her tea. "Birney used to be a slaveholder. Then he freed his slaves. For a time he believed like Father that all slaves should be returned to Africa and colonized. But I think he's given up that idea. He is a brilliant man and has a degree from Princeton. Right now he's establishing the Huntsville Female Academy. He wanted me to recommend some teachers." She poured some tea into Harriet's cup. "I recommended Miss Brown, Miss Southmayd, and Miss Baldwin. I don't know if he'll call them."

"How old is he?"

"He's a little younger than I am—"

"Mmmm. That means he's in his late twenties."

"Hattie, I'm not interested in marriage if that's what you're thinking. My whole heart is wrapped up in one idea: female education! Just think, in our time women never go to college; they're not allowed to vote; and those who do work are confined to the most menial jobs. I'm working eight days a week for the time when there'll be women doctors, women lawyers, women senators. Moreover, I'm prepared to lead the way."

Harriet laughed. "You sound just like Pa and all the other Beechers. All of you are determined to change the world—"

"And why not? If God be for us, who can be against us! We have a big job to do and we all must do our part." Catherine stood up. "Not to change the subject, but, Hattie, I've been wondering if you have seen that poem about Old Ironsides? It seems to have been republished in all the newspapers."

"Yes, I've seen it and I think it's great. Do you think it'll save the old ship?"

"I don't know. It may. Words, Hattie, have power. And when properly put together words have dynamic power. John even wrote, 'In the beginning was the Word' (John 1:1)."

As summer eased into fall and fall hardened into winter,

Harriet kept praying that God would show her what she was to do with her life. But even though she reminded the Lord that she was going on twenty, the only response she received was that she should keep going. In addition to this frustration, she failed to attract the attention of a single young man. She changed her hairdos, and even acted as if she were as dull as everyone else. Nothing worked. Her only joyful companion was Georgiana.

When school let out, Harriet returned to Boston. There, she learned that her father had endured a seeming-tragedy. The Hanover meetinghouse had burned to the ground. "It could have been saved," lamented Lyman, "but the firemen refused to use any of their equipment. A friend told me they just stood in front and let her burn. And while she burned, they mocked me by singing:

> While Beecher's church holds out to burn,
> The vilest sinner may return.

"It was a terrible fire; and one of the things that made it worse was that without knowing it, a merchant who'd rented one of the missionary rooms had packed it full of liquor. The alcohol made the fire so hot the steeple split in two."

"And what happened to the organ?"

"It fell into the flames and is completely gone."

"That's terrible."

"We've been using a rented building. But we have full insurance and we'll rebuild." Suddenly he began to laugh. "After she had burned to the ground, I happened to be in a bookstore. There I remarked, 'Well, my old jug's broke, just been to see it.' Instead of laughing, the people stared at me as if I were insane."

Harriet frowned as she studied her father. Finally she said, "Papa, you used to get the hypos every three or four months. How could you have been so casual when the meetinghouse was utterly destroyed?"

"Easy. I'm doing the work of the Lord. And, Hattie, I've learned across the years that if one is doing the work of the Lord, he need not worry. God is sovereign!"

While Lyman Beecher was awaiting a formal call to Cincinnati, William Lloyd Garrison was hurriedly laying the foundation for his attack on slavery. With the smell of ink on his hands and the music of a rumbling press in his heart, he decided that his best move was to publish a radical newspaper which would unite the abolitionists, inspire the slaves—and convert the masses to his way of thinking.

Garrison had no money, but that didn't stop him. He persuaded the foreman of the *Christian Examiner* to lend him their type in exchange for a day's work. Since the type had to be returned the next day, he had to compose the copy at night, print the paper, replace the type into their trays, and return them in the morning. But having an oversupply of adrenaline, a twenty-four-hour day on an empty stomach didn't bother him.

With his words formed like a hatchet, Garrison set the type for his first editorial in the *Liberator*. Determining the tone for what was to follow, he wrote:

> On this subject, I do not wish to think, or speak, or write, with moderation. No! no! Tell a man whose house is on fire to give a moderate alarm; tell him to moderately rescue his wife from the hands of the ravisher; tell the mother to gradually extricate her babe from the fire into which it has fallen—but urge me not to use moderation in a cause like the present. I am in earnest—I will not equivocate—I will not excuse—I will not retreat a single inch—AND I WILL BE HEARD.

That first issue was printed on a format that measured fourteen by nine and a quarter inches. There were only 400 copies; and the editorial, appearing on page one, was slightly askew. (By the end of two years it had only attained fifty subscribers.) But the small circulation didn't worry Garrison. He knew that a small flame can start a big fire. And he determined to start a big fire.

With incredible genius for publicity, Garrison mailed copies to those papers he knew disagreed with him—especially to those in the deep south. Many southern editors denounced him with heated invective. Others could use strong language, but few could match Garrison. In answer to one editorial, he replied, "My contempt of it is unutterable. Nothing but my own death, or want of patronage, shall stop the *Liberator*."

Arthur Tappan, a New York City businessman who had earned a fortune with cash-and-carry stores, was attracted to Garrison and supplied him with the necessary funds.

Garrison did not believe in violence; and he denounced those who did. But when on August 31, 1831, a group of from fifty to seventy-five slaves who had been inspired by the black prophet, Nat Turner, went on a rampage in Virginia and killed sixty-one whites, many pointed fingers at Garrison.

Lyman Beecher was aware of all these things, but his heart was set on establishing a seminary in Cincinnati, and that project claimed his full attention. The agent of the projected seminary was satisfied that Lyman Beecher was the only one who could make the school a success. He had written to his superiors:

> After much consultation it appeared to be the common impression . . . that Doctor Beecher of Boston, if he could be obtained, would be the best man. That, as he is the most prominent, popular and powerful preacher in the nation, he would immediately give character elevation and success to our seminary, draw together young men from every part of our country, secure the confidence and cooperation of the ministers and churches both east and west of the Alleghany Mountains, and awaken a general interest in the old state in behalf of the West.

Beecher was excited by the call. Still, persuaded by his congregation that he must remain with them until the building was completed, he declined. The following year he was approached again. This time it was explained that Arthur Tappan, the man who was supporting Garrison's *Liberator*, had offered a large sum for the seminary, provided Beecher could be secured to be president.

Lyman was flattered. Yet he had a problem. "I should exceedingly depreciate the annual drilling of a class one year in biblical literature, the next in theology, and lastly in composition and eloquence—one stratum of knowledge piled on another without any cement between is about as wise as if a man should eat his meat one day, his vegetables the next, and his pies and cake on the third." He then went on to explain that he would like to pastor a congregation while he was also serving as president of the seminary.

All of this was agreeable to the trustees; and so, in due time, it was arranged for Beecher to also be the pastor of the Second Presbyterian Church of Cincinnati. Lyman was excited by his opportunity, but since all arrangements had been by mail, and since his acceptance meant severing all that was dear to him, he decided to take Catherine with him and view the city with his own eyes before he made his ultimate decision. Boarding a stage in Boston, they went to Wheeling, and then from there took a riverboat down the Ohio to Cincinnati.

With both her father and oldest sister gone, Harriet succumbed to an acute state of hypochondria. Almost wishing she were dead, she called on Georgiana. "Everyone is making a success but me," she wailed.

"You're only twenty-two," comforted her friend.

"Yes, I'm twenty-two!" She nodded her head vigorously. "What have I accomplished? Nothing. Absolutely nothing. Zero. I've never even had a date. I'm just an unwanted, good-for-nothing nobody. Oh, yes, I've accomplished one thing. I'm an expert hat-finder."

They both laughed.

"Sarah didn't have her baby until she was ninety."

"Maybe so, but she was beautiful and was married when she was quite young. Mary became the mother of Jesus when she was in her teens and Joan of Arc threw the English out of France before she was eighteen."

Georgiana stood up. "Let me brew you some tea. That'll make you feel better. Then I'll fix your hair. Any suggestions?"

"Yes. Part it in the center, sweep it to the back of my head, and make a lot of ringlets. I'll then put a metal band over the top of my forehead."

"Are you teasing?" Georgiana frowned.

"No, I'm no teasing. I know that'll make me look as if I'm in my thirties." She sighed. "But what's the difference? I'm not even a has-been. I'm a never was!"

Two hours after Georgiana had started, Harriet was the proud possessor of a dozen curls—six on each side. After peering in the mirror, Harriet remarked, "You did a good job, considering what you had to work with."

Catherine was delighted with Cincinnati. In a letter to Harriet she expressed her enthusiasm. "We reached here in three days from Wheeling. The next day father and I with three gentlemen walked out to Walnut Hills. The site of the seminary is very beautiful and picturesque, though I was disappointed to find that both the river and city are hidden by intervening hills. I never saw a place so capable as being rendered a Paradise. The seminary is located on a farm of one hundred and twenty acres of fine land, with groves of trees around it.

"It seems to me that everybody I used to know is here or coming here. Besides our two uncles, there is Ned King, an old Litchfield beau, and Mother's own cousin, now General King; Cousin E. Tuthill; Abraham Chittenden's family from Guilford; Mrs. James Butler, from Litchfield; Mr. and Mrs.

Bingham, with whom we used to board at Dr. Strong's, and diverse others.

"Yesterday Father preached in the morning and evening to crowded houses.

"As to Father, I never saw such a field of usefulness and influences as is offered here. I see no difficulties or objections; everything is ready and everybody gives a welcome except Dr. Wilson's folks, and they are finding that it is wisest and best to be still, and we hope that before a great while they will be *friendly*. Father is determined to get acquainted with Dr. Wilson, and to be *friendly* with him, and I think he will succeed."

As Harriet read and reread that last paragraph she wondered why Catherine had underlined the word "friendly." In her heart, she knew that one of the reasons her father was anxious to leave Boston was to escape the Unitarians. Could it be that he would be stepping from the skillet into the fire? Trying not be pessimistic, she folded the letter and filed it away in her drawer.

12

Cincinnati

With customary skill at generating enthusiasm, Dr. Beecher persuaded all of his available children that Cincinnati was the Jerusalem of the Promised Land, and that they should move there immediately.

Five Beechers found the move impossible. Married to Thomas C. Perkins, a successful lawyer, Mary Foote was firmly established in Hartford. William H. was busy in his first pastorate in Rhode Island. Charles and Henry Ward were completing their schooling in the East, while Edward was already in the West, serving as president of Illinois College in Jacksonville.

Although five could not go, the remaining nine were most eager to be a part of the Beecher invasion of the West. Those nine were Lyman, his wife, Esther (his half sister), Catherine, Harriet and George, together with the second Mrs. Beecher's children: Isabella, Thomas, and James. According to the preacher's plans, they would first travel to New York City where he would set out to raise two twenty-thousand-dollar endowments in order to produce the income to support two additional professors, one of which was to be Calvin Stowe.

The City, sometimes referred to as Babylon on the Hudson, fascinated all the Beechers—especially Harriet. In a letter, she wrote: "Father is all in his own element, dipping into books; consulting authorities for his oration, going round here and there, begging, borrowing and spoiling the Egyptians, delighted with past success and confident of the future."

From New York City, the Beecher "troops" raided Philadelphia. There, Dr. Beecher spoke to packed churches, contacted rich men, and raised more money. Although weary of all the hurry, the clan became more enthusiastic by the day. As their train puffed out of the City of Brotherly Love, twenty-three-year-old George started all the Beechers singing; and a little later he got them distributing tracts. At an inn in Downington, about thirty miles east of Philadelphia, Harriet addressed a letter to Georgiana.

"Here we all are," she wrote. "Noah and his wife and his sons and daughters, with cattle and creeping things, all dropped down in front of this tavern. If today is a fair specimen of our journey, it will be very pleasant: obliging driver, good roads, good spirits, good dinner, fine scenery, and now and then some psalms and hymns and spiritual songs."

Several homes in Wheeling were opened to them and the churches were crowded where Lyman spoke. But all was not tranquility. The newspapers screamed with the story that Cincinnati had been stricken with an epidemic of cholera. "The streets are covered with a pall of smoke," reported a recent escapee. "They are burning bituminous coal so that the smoke will kill the disease. I saw stacks and stacks of coffins."

"What are we to do?" asked Mrs. Beecher, concern written on her face.

"We'll remain in Wheeling until the panic is over," assured Lyman. "The Lord will direct our steps."

The local Congregational and Presbyterian congregations were delighted that the Beechers would remain. Even though Beecher's New Light theology seemed a little strange, the people filled the meetinghouses, made pledges, and enrolled their sons in the new seminary.

While they awaited news that the epidemic had abated, Harriet became excited over a news item in one of the papers. "Listen to this," she cried. "Old Ironsides will be spared!"

Startled, Lyman grabbed the paper. Out loud, he read the item: "Due to pressure brought about by the reprinting of Oliver Wendell Holmes' poem, 'Old Ironsides,' in newspapers all over the country, the Navy has decided to save The Constitution."

After folding the paper and swatting a fly that had settled on Harriet's shoulder, he concluded, "That shows the power of the pen."

"But we still have dueling even though they printed forty thousand copies of your sermon," commented Harriet somewhat mockingly.

Beecher held up his palms. "Ah, but remember the Bible says: 'Cast thy bread upon the waters: for thou shalt find it after many days' (Eccles. 11:1)." A confident smile brightened his face.

"Maybe so, but Andrew Jackson, the man who killed his enemy in a duel, is still president," scoffed Harriet.

"Don't you have faith?"

"I do. I'm just teasing."

Following two weeks of waiting, the news from Cincinnati was that the epidemic was lifting. Encouraged by this, Lyman chartered a stagecoach to complete the journey. Packed with Beechers and their luggage, the coach jolted southward on a rut-filled, pothole-filled, corrugated road that paralleled the Ohio. In one particular stretch where the coach alternately swayed, bounced, shuddered, got stuck in the mud, and slipped into ditches, Mrs. Beecher eventually asked, "Dearest, why could we not have sailed down the river?"

"Because I wanted us to all be alone and together as a single unit," replied Lyman. "Besides, a little shaking is good for us. It's good for our dyspepsia. In addition, it's free and *it'll help shake the devil out of us*," he laughed.

Each problem of the journey recorded an indelible memory in Harriet's mind. Years later, she used her memory to brighten a story. She described a region in the West "where the mud is of unfathomable and sublime depth, roads are made of round, rough logs, arranged transversely side by side, and then coated with earth, turf, and whatsoever may come to hand." She also wrote about "the interesting process of pulling down rail fences to pry their carriages out of mudholes."

The difficulties of the way, however, did not squelch all the Beecher optimism and joy. George inspired them to sing even in the roughest places, and when occasion arose they continued to hand out tracts.

Finally, the stagecoach reached Cincinnati on Wednesday, November 14, 1832. Uncle Samuel and Uncle John were prepared to receive them, so all of the Beechers had a comfortable place in which to relax after their long, tiring journey from Wheeling. The smell of smoke from the fire that had been kept burning on numerous street corners in order to dissipate the cholera was still pungent in the air as uniformed blacks carried the Beechers' luggage into their assigned rooms.

While waiting for supper, Harriet noticed an advertisement in bold type on an inside page of a newspaper. Her eyes widened as she read:

NOTICE

> The undersigned, having an excellent pack of HOUNDS for trailing and catching runaway slaves, informs the public that his prices in the future will be as follows: For each day employed in hunting or trailing . . . 2 dollars and fifty cents.
>
> For catching slaves . . . 10 dollars. For going over ten miles and catching slaves . . . 20 dollars.
>
> If sent for, the above prices will be exacted in cash. The subscriber resides one and a half miles south of Dadeville, Alabama.

Not believing what she read, Harriet said, "Uncle Samuel, is that sort of thing going on *now*?"

"It is. A friend mailed me that paper from Alabama. But even though Alabama is a long way from here, Kentucky is right across the river. Kentucky is a slave state. Let me show you an advertisement that I clipped out of a Kentucky paper." He withdrew a clipping from his billfold. Harriet felt her heart jump as she scanned the notice.

$750 REWARD!

> RAN AWAY from my plantation on the 10th of June, a family of five slaves.
>
> Jim is about 22. His wife, Mary, is about 23. Mary's mother is a very black woman about 60. She has white hair and is stooped. Jim and Mary are quadroons and may pretend they are white. Jim has the letter T branded in his left palm. Their twin girls are about 3 and are also nearly white. Jim and Mary are very intelligent. They can even read.
>
> I will give the above award to anyone who will bring the entire family to me. Or I will pay $75 for the securing of any one of them—dead or alive.
>
> Elijah Dent
> Nashville, Tenn.

Trying to keep her voice calm, Harriet asked, "Uncle Samuel, what's a quadroon?"

"A quadroon is a slave with three white grandparents."

"How could that be?"

"Don't you remember the story of your aunt, my sister Mary? She married John Hubbard, a Jamaica planter. When she got to Jamaica she learned that he had fathered a houseful of mulatto children, and that he considered these children his slaves. She was so horrified she left him."

"I remember stories about her. But I was only two when she died." Handing the clipping back to her uncle, she asked another question. "Since slavery is so wicked, why isn't it stopped?"

"Oh, but everyone doesn't think it's wicked! There are many kind slaveholders. Freed slaves have even returned to their masters and asked to be slaves again. Also, there are freed blacks who own their own slaves; and some of *them* are hardhearted."

Harriet shook her head. "There may be kind slavers. Still, slavery is a wicked business."

"I agree. And yet many slavers feel that they are doing the work of the Lord—"

"The work of the Lord?"

"Yes, the work of the Lord! The biggest slave ship in the days of Queen Elizabeth was the *Jesus*, and another was the *John the Baptist.* Many slavers had their slaves baptized before they branded them and loaded them in their ships."

"How horrible!"

"Do you like the hymn, *Amazing Grace*?"

"Of course."

"It was written by John Newton, a former slaver."

"Everyone knows that."

"Yes, but everyone does not know that Newton continued to slave for a long time *after* he was converted."

"After he was converted?" Harriet gasped.

"Yes, after. Sometimes he studied his Bible on his knees in the cabin of his ship while the slaves he had just purchased were screaming in terror as they were being branded."

"That's dreadful!"

Their conversation was interrupted by the butler. "Dinner has been served," said the magnificently uniformed black.

All of the Beechers with the exception of Harriet allowed their plates to be refilled. "Harriet, is anything wrong?" asked her stepmother.

"I—I'm afraid I don't feel very well," replied Harriet.

Harriet enjoyed walking around the city, going down to the docks, watching the slaves whose Kentucky masters rented them out to people in the city. Everything seemed so new and interesting. But she didn't like the sight of the pigs that roamed the streets and left their droppings in whatever place they happened to be. While she and the others were still unsettled, awaiting a place to live, she wrote to her sister in Hartford. "I have much solicitude on Jamie's account," she referred to her four-year-old stepbrother, James, "lest he should form improper intimacies, for yesterday we saw him parading by the house with his arm over the neck of a great hog, apparently on the most amicable terms; and the other day he actually got on the back of one, and rode some distance. So much for allowing these animals to promenade the streets, a particular in which Mrs. Cincinnati has imitated the domestic arrangements of some of her elder sisters, and a very disgusting one it is."

Eventually the Beechers moved into a rental while they awaited the completion of their permanent home. Although Mrs. Beecher hated Cincinnati, she delighted that at least her temporary home was not infected with rats as was the house in Litchfield. Nonetheless, the house which they rented from an old bachelor had problems. Harriet expounded on those problems in a letter to Georgiana.

It is the "most inconvenient, ill-arranged, good-for-nothing, and altogether to be execrated affair that was ever put together. The kitchen is so disposed that it cannot be reached from any part of the house without going into the air. Mother is actually obliged to put on a bonnet and cloak every time she goes into it. In the house are two parlors with folding doors between them. The back parlor has but one window and has its lower half painted to keep out what light there is."

The housing didn't bother Lyman. "Cincinnati," he exulted, "wasn't even incorporated until 1802; and, already in its mere thirty years of existence, it has 30,000 inhabitants—and is still growing." The preacher had a right to be proud, for the young city had ten hotels, forty churches, forty-seven doctors, fifty-six lawyers. Also, there were hospitals, medical schools, and sixty-four weekly mails. (Seventeen arrived by steamboat, eleven by post riders, and thirty-six by stage.) Likewise, there was a fire department which was equipped with hand-pump engines, cisterns filled with emergency water, and wooden mains to transport the water. Better yet, the wooden mains belonged to his brothers-in-law, John P. and Samuel Foote!

Cincinnati was proud of the forthcoming Lane Seminary, so named in honor of the man who had donated the land. It was also proud of the new president and his distinguished daughter, Catherine. One paper boasted that other than Ben Franklin, Lyman Beecher was the most quoted man in America.

Beecher enjoyed his celebrity, even though he knew that the Reverend D. Joshua Lacy Wilson, an Old School Calvinist, and pastor of the First Presbyterian Church, had been so opposed to his appointment he had resigned from the seminary board. Still, as uninhibited as ever, he, the Big Gun of Calvinism, was not afraid to express his views whenever and wherever he chose to express them.

Beecher despised Andrew Jackson, and his reelection that November didn't improve his support for him. The fact that he was a duelist and had bullets of antagonists within his body was like a malignancy in Beecher's system. Nonetheless, his loyalty to the Bible meant that he should pray for him. On a certain Sunday morning, Harriet was delighted to hear him pray, "Oh, Lord, grant that we may not despise our rulers—and grant that they may not act *so we can't help it.*"

Somewhat to her dismay, Catherine discovered that the people in Cincinnati were determined that she, according to them, an authority, should launch a female academy in their midst. She also found that a children's book on geography was desperately needed. Physically exhausted from winding up her affairs in Hartford, she realized that she did not have the strength to undertake both projects at the same time. Ah, but she did have a reliable helper!

Approaching Harriet who was busy mending Jamie's pants, she said, "Hattie, how would you like to write a children's book on geography?"

Harriet made a final stitch as she considered the question. Then, after tucking her needle in a spare patch, she replied, "I'd love to, provided I could use my imagination and make it readable."

Catherine explained both the age and page requirements and Harriet got busy. With access to her father's library and other books, she kept her pen flying. The pages piled up. Soon the modest little book was finished. Within weeks it was accepted by a reliable Cincinnati publisher. The publisher paid cash. Harriet's share was $187. This was the first money she had earned as a writer and she was elated. On March 8, 1833, she noticed an advertisement in the Cincinnati papers. It read:

A NEW GEOGRAPHY
For Children

Corey & Fairbank have in the press
and will publish in a few days, a
GEOGRAPHY FOR CHILDREN
with numerous maps, and engravings,
upon an improved plan
BY CATHERINE E. BEECHER

Puzzled that her name was not in the ad, Harriet felt a stab of disappointment. Then she realized that although she had written the book, it had, indeed, been based on Catherine's plan. With great effort, she tried to console herself that she had not been slighted.

But deep inside, she knew it wasn't quite fair.

13

Semi-Colon Club

When Harriet was asked to join the Semi-Colon Club shortly after her arrival in Cincinnati, she had no idea that the club, along with at least three of its members, would completely change her life. The major thing that impressed her was the club's rather odd name.

Among the members was a rising attorney by the name of Salmon P. Chase. Throughout the city, this slightly balding, square-faced young man, a mere three years older than Harriet, was known for his fairness. But since he defended so many runaways, Kentucky slaveholders sneered at him as "the attorney general of fugitive slaves."

Calvin Stowe and his wife Eliza, daughter of the president of Dartmouth, were also members. Harriet was especially attracted to Eliza. In a letter to Georgiana, she wrote: "Let me introduce you to Mrs. Stowe, a delicate pretty, little woman, with hazel eyes, auburn hair, fair complexion, fine color, a pretty little mouth, and a most interesting simplicity and timidity of manner."

Calvin, a short, stocky man, whose wide face seemed even wider because of soft sideburns, was nine years older than Harriet. He had taught at Bowdoin College, his alma mater, and at Dartmouth. He was now Professor of Biblical Literature at Lane and was famous all over America for his scholarship.

Harriet was intrigued by the way he shortened *expect* to *'spect*. In some of his idiosyncrasies, he reminded her of her father.

But perhaps the most prominent member of the Semi-

Colon Club was Judge James Hall, a writer and editor of the new *Western Monthly Magazine*. The group met each Monday night at 7:30 in Samuel Foote's home. During normal routine, a reader was elected at the beginning of the session. This reader then read stories written by the members. Some were signed. Others were anonymous. Then, after a period of discussion, refreshments were served.

Harriet wrote numerous anonymous selections and was flattered to hear the word genius used during the period of comment. Encouraged, she was excited when Judge Hall offered a prize of fifty dollars for the best story submitted by November 10. When that date came and nothing suitable had been turned in, he advanced the deadline to February 1, 1834.

Pondering over her New England days and the stories her father had told her about Uncle Lot, she secured a fresh pen and began to write. The title was easy. She wrote: A NEW ENGLAND SKETCH by Miss Harriet E. Beecher. The opening lines were also easy:

> And I am to write a story—but of what, and where? Shall it be radiant with the sky of Italy? or eloquent with the beau ideal of Greece? Shall it breathe odor languor from the Orient, or chivalry from the Occident? or gayety from France, or vigor from England? No, no; these are too old—too romance-like—too obviously picturesque for me. No; let me turn to my own land—my own New England; the land of bright fires and strong hearts; the land of deeds and not of words. . . .[1]

As she labored on her story, visualizing the prize and imagining what it would be like in the *Western Monthly Magazine*, she hoped that if she were successful, her name would be used. Moreover, she had cause to hope because when Hall reviewed the geography book in his magazine, he had noted that it was by C. & H. Beecher. The sight of that "& H." sent excitement racing down her spine.

Finally, the story finished, she turned it in. She now had to wait until February 1 to learn the result. And that seemed a dozen eternities away. The time, however, flew by quickly as Catherine kept her busy at her new school. In addition, Theodore Weld, an abolitionist enrolled at Lane, was in the

---

[1]When republished in her collection of stories entitled *Mayflower*, it was renamed Uncle Tim. Later, in the Houghton Mifflin edition, it was changed to Uncle Lot.

process of turning the student body of nearly one hundred into fire-eating abolitionists.

Converted under the ministry of lawyer-turned-evangelist Charles G. Finney, thirty-one-year-old Weld was just as dynamic as his spiritual father. In addition, he concentrated his immense talent into one channel: *immediate abolition.* Inspired by the fact that Cincinnati was just across the river from legal slavery, he determined that the seminary was to be both a terminal in the Underground Railroad and a publishing center for all abolitionists.

At the time he enrolled at Lane, he was the only dedicated abolitionist in the school. Most of the students felt that slavery was wrong, but none of them were quite certain how the system could be changed. There was, however, a colonization society, and many of the students were at least moderately active within this organization.

Weld decided that he would change all of this. Having discovered that William T. Allan, a native of Alabama, had been raised by a slaveholder and was scheduled to inherit slaves, he pursued this friendship. After turning Allan into an abolitionist, he and his convert went after the others. Soon, a large portion of the student body was enrolled in their cause. At this point, Weld approached Dr. Beecher. "We'd like to debate this subject," he said.

Beecher thought it was a good idea and the debates were announced. The *Lane Debates*, as history knows them, continued for eighteen nights. Harriet attended most of them and was deeply impressed. James Bradley, a black student, kept the audience in tears as he related how he had been brought to the United States on a slaver when he was a child; how he was sold to a South Carolina planter, and how that planter had allowed him to work out his freedom.

James A. Thome, a native of Kentucky, told how degrading slavery was to the sons of the planters and sought to prove his point with stirring anecdotes. Others, from various parts of the South, made additional statements—all dramatic.

After the abolitionists had dominated the floor for nine days, the colonizers were given the remaining nine days. But their arguments were neither dramatic nor convincing. At the end of the debates, almost all the students were convinced abolitionists. Elated, Weld wrote to Lewis Tappan, brother of Arthur, "We believe that faith without *works* is dead. We have formed a large efficient organization for elevating the colored people of Cincinnati."

Influenced by Finney, Weld believed that action should be preceded by thorough research. After studying the problem, he informed Lewis Tappan: "Of the almost 3000 blacks in Cincinnati more than three-fourths of the adults are emancipated slaves who worked out their own freedom. I visited this week about 30 families, and found that some members of more than half these families are still in bondage, and the father and children struggling to lay up money enough to purchase their freedom. I found one man who had just finished paying for his wife and five children. Another man and wife who bought themselves some years ago, have been working day and night to purchase their children; they had just redeemed the last! and had paid for themselves and children 1400 dollars! But I cannot tell half, and must stop. After spending three or four hours, and getting facts, I was forced to stop from sheer heartache and agony."[2]

Weld's concern about the blacks was so overwhelming, he devoted every moment he could spare to them. He remembered: "If I ate in the city it was at *their* tables. If I slept in the city it was in *their* homes. If I attended parties, it was *theirs*; weddings—*theirs*; funerals—*theirs*; religious meetings—*theirs*. . . . During the 18 months I spent at Lane Seminary I did not attend Doctor Beecher's Church once."[3]

President Beecher had no racial prejudice. Blacks had lived in his home. But he was a realist and was sensitive to the mores of the times. The seminary was in a precarious financial condition and he did not want to jeopardize its success in any way. He summoned Weld into his office.

"You are taking just the course to defeat your own object," he said in his fatherly way. "If you want to teach colored schools, I can fill your pockets with money; but if you visit colored families, and walk with them in the streets, you will be overwhelmed."

Weld listened respectfully. But he did not agree. His differences with Beecher continued to widen. One night they argued until 2 a.m. without coming to agreement or reaching the slightest compromise.

Watching the dissenting fires growing from a distance, Harriet was concerned. But her main focus remained on whether or not she had won that fifty dollar prize. Waiting

---

[2]Weld-Grimké Letters, 1, 135. As quoted from *Crusader of Freedom*, by Theodore Weld, p. 73.
[3]Ibid. 1, 273. As quoted from *Crusader of Freedom*, p. 74.

for February 1 to arrive was almost as painful as it had been to await July 4 when she was a child. Finally, the great day arrived. After fixing her hair in a manner to increase her height, she dressed in her finest and headed for the Semi-Colon Club.

Uncle Samuel's house was unusually crowded that evening and Harriet felt a tense feeling of anticipation as she awaited the outcome. After what seemed to her an eternity, Judge Hall stood up. Obviously enjoying the suspense, he prolonged it as much as possible by mentioning the past accomplishments of the club and outlining what he hoped the members would be enabled to accomplish in the future. Then, after removing his spectacles and carefully polishing each lense, he coughed, and acknowledged, "Several of the submissions were unusually fine. They showed strong, native ability. The best one, however, was the one submitted by Harriet Elizabeth Beecher. Will the winner kindly step forward."

Harriet was so excited she almost tripped on her long dress. And her hand trembled as she reached for the fifty dollar check. After thanking Judge Hall, she faced the members. "This is one of the happiest days of my life. I now have a request. I wish all of you would pray that the Lord would guide my life and my pen so that I can be useful in His kingdom."

The story, renamed *A New England Tale*, was the lead story in the April issue of the *Western Monthly Magazine*, filling the entire front page. Her name, Harriet Elizabeth Beecher, had been printed at the top in bold type. Skipping from cloud to cloud, she now dreamed of the future. Within minutes she placed on her desk a new sheet of blank paper.

Quickly, she wrote the title *Aunt Mary*, and began to compose. The first paragraph was easy:

> Since sketching character is the mode, I too take up my pencil, not to make you laugh, though peradventure it may be—to get you to sleep.

After the story was completed, she personally handed it to Judge Hall. Then she spent an almost sleepless night. Would it be accepted? It was. Again there was a fresh check in her hand.

Two stories in a row in the West's leading magazine meant that she had talent! As she smiled at her gray-blue eyes in the mirror, a daring thought widened her smile. Could it be that she might, just might, be another Sir Walter Scott?

Harriet's confidence in herself increased by the day. True, the boys continued to shun her; and she remained the runt of the family. Nonetheless, she was a writer—and her words were being read all over America. Yes, God was opening a door for her to step through. Perhaps the time would come when she would even exchange letters and greetings with the great writers of the world. Her ecstasy, however, came to an abrupt end when she opened the May issue of the *Western Monthly Magazine.*

There, before her, was a vicious attack on the student body at Lane. Obviously incensed at the way the students were fraternizing with the blacks, the writer used such colorful words as "embryo clergymen," "precocious undergraduates" and accused them of uttering "sophomoric declamations." When she showed the column to her father, he became very upset.

"Maybe we should not have had those debates," suggested Harriet.

"You may be right," replied her father.

Infuriated, Weld replied to the attack in a column in the *Cincinnati Journal.* Following some strong, defensive words, he asked: "Whom does it behoove to keep his heart in contact with the woes and guilt of a perishing world if not the student who is preparing for the ministry?" He concluded: "Through the grace of God, the history of the next five years will teach this lesson to the most reluctant learner."[4]

Although Ohio was not a slave state, Cincinnati had a large proslavery element; and this group was so stirred by what the students were doing that many of them threatened to march on the school. Alarmed, Lyman Beecher faced the entire student body. Using carefully chosen words, he assured them that they were right, slavery was wrong, the blacks should be helped; but, he insisted, they were ahead of their time. He advised them to go slowly and quoted Ecclesiastes 1:1—"To everything there is a season, and a time to every purpose under the heaven."

The more radical of the student-abolitionists disagreed. Elizur Wright sneered: "The young men . . . were not guilty of doing wrong, but of doing *right* TOO SOON."[5]

Hoping to calm the tempest, Beecher mounted his pulpit

---

[4]*Liberator*, June 14, 1834.

[5]Annual Report of the American Antislavery Society, 1835. Both quotes from *Crusader of Freedom*, p. 77.

in the Second Presbyterian Church and preached on why he believed in the colonization of the slaves. The sermon was impressive, but many of the citizens with slave-owning relatives across the river in Kentucky were not impressed.

When summer came, all of the faculty with the exception of Calvin left in order to rest and raise money for the school. Beecher hoped that during the summer vacation calm would be restored to both the school and the city. His hopes were in vain. Since many of the students could not afford to go home, they remained in Cincinnati and spent most of their time cultivating and aiding the blacks. As they visited in their homes, attended their churches, walked with them down the streets, and were guests at their tables, the flames beneath the proslavery boiler of discontent flamed higher and became more intense. Bystanders looked on awaiting the inevitable explosion.

Dismayed, Harriet knew that she had to get out of Cincinnati for a while in order to retain her sanity. Henry Ward's impending graduation from Amherst that June provided the excuse. After making a new dress, she took the stage to Toledo, crossed Lake Erie by steamboat, transferred to another stage at Buffalo, and continued on to Massachusetts.

Harriet was delighted to learn that although Henry Ward had not graduated at the top of his class, he had overcome his thickness of speech, was very popular—and had become an effective preacher. She was also happy to learn that he would be enrolling at Lane that fall.

While visiting relatives, stopping at Niagara Falls, and viewing other sites, Harriet received a letter filled with disturbing news. Cholera had again broken out in Cincinnati and Eliza Stowe was not well. Remembering the fine times she had had with the little woman with the hazel eyes, Harriet felt impelled to pray for her. A few days later, a letter arrived with the news that Eliza had died. Back in Cincinnati, Harriet called on Calvin to comfort him.

"When I knew that she was stricken, I wept out loud," said Calvin. Removing his spectacles he wiped his eyes. "But Eliza—God bless her!—Eliza murmured, 'Don't weep for me. Just repeat the 14th and 15th chapters of John.' While I was doing that, her eyes followed each movement of my lips. As the end drew near, she exclaimed, 'Oh, joy—joy unspeakable and full of glory—full of glory!' Her final words were, 'I am a lamb.' I believe, Hattie, she must have been thinking about the 23rd psalm. It was one of her favorite psalms."

As they continued to visit, Calvin pointed to a large portrait of Eliza hanging on the wall. "I'll never forget her," he murmured. "She was the angel of my life."

Calvin Stowe had other reasons as well to be discouraged. During the middle of August, some of the extreme abolitionist students had staged a party for black women on the Lane campus. This had so enraged the public; some had threatened to burn the school down. Alarmed, the Board of Trustees had decreed that the Lane Anti-Slavery Society, created by Weld, was no more. They also insisted that the slavery issue should not be discussed in any of the seminary rooms—not even across the table at mealtime. Moreover, to enforce their restrictions, and to let the public know what was being done, they published their restrictions in the *Cincinnati Daily Gazette.*

This hot news item was copied by other papers throughout the nation. Eventually, William Lloyd Garrison denounced the school in *The Liberator.* He wrote: "Lane Seminary is now to be regarded as strictly a Bastile of oppression—a spiritual Inquisition."

Weld's response was to persuade his followers to live in tents in the nearby hills. "We will remain here," he announced, "until we find a school which permits freedom of speech." Aggravated by what was taking place at Lane, Arthur Tappan, now a dedicated abolitionist, provided funds to open a theological department in Oberlin College, a revived school in Oberlin, Ohio, just south of Lake Erie. The new department was to be headed by Charles G. Finney, Weld's spiritual father and the most renowned evangelist in the world. A prominent feature of the new department was that it was open to all "irrespective of color."

Feeling he was on Mt. Pisgah, Weld inspired his followers to enroll at Oberlin for the next term.

Informed about what was taking place in Cincinnati, President Beecher eventually broke away from his money-raising trips and returned to the seminary. He firmly believed that he could cleanse the wound, and that Lane would influence the entire West. He was sadly mistaken. Nonetheless, he continued on as president even though many classrooms were nearly empty.

That October, he approached Harriet. "The Cincinnati Synod is meeting at Ripley," he informed her. "Why don't you come along? John Rankin has invited us to stay in his home—"

"Is he the preacher who keeps a light burning in his home in order to help escaping slaves?" Harriet's eyes widened.

"He is. And other than Levi Coffin, he knows more about the Underground Railroad than anyone. Professor Stowe will be staying with us—"

"But will there be room?" Harriet asked.

"Of course. Rankin may even tell you how he helped Eliza after she crossed the Ohio on the ice. It was a hair-raising experience."

"Then I'm going with you!" exclaimed Harriet. "That material might—just might—give me an idea for an article, or, perhaps, a short story."

14
The Underground Railroad

The sun was nearing the horizon when Harriet, along with her father and Calvin Stowe, stepped into the Rankin house—a small brick building perched on a cliff overlooking the river.[1]

"Welcome! Welcome!" greeted the plump lady of the house. "You're just in time for supper. John and I've been counting the hours until you'd get here. But before we go to the table, let me show you your rooms." She led the way to a tiny chamber just off the kitchen. "This is for Dr. Beecher and Professor Stowe." Then she opened another door next to the porch on the south side. "And this, Harriet, will be your room." She pointed out the window to the river. As Harriet followed her finger, she saw the broad stream just beneath them.

"Is that where Eliza crossed on the ice?" ventured Harriet.

"It is. I'll never forget the day she came. The old river was a-groanin' with huge chunks of ice slammin' into each other. We could hear 'em a-rumblin' even up here."

"How did she cross?"

"She just leaped from one chunk to another."

"Weren't they slippery?" Harriet stared.

"Reckon they were. She fell several times. But Eliza was a determined gal. When she got here her feet and knees were all bloody and she'd lost her shawl. We almost ran out of bandages—"

"Was she alone?"

"Oh, no. She had a young'un. Poor thing. He was shiverin'

[1]The Rankin house is still standing.

with the cold. Excuse me while I light the lantern. I imagine you're 'bout to starve." She tightened her apron and went out on the porch. Harriet watched as she lit the wick of a heavy lantern. "What's that for?" she asked.

"To show 'em where the house is." She spoke in a matter-of-fact way.

"Will any come tonight?"

"Maybe. We've already had over five hundred.[2] If they come, just ignore 'em. John will know what to do. But we'd better stop talkin' and start eatin'."

Harriet had many more questions, but she forced herself to keep still as she thoughtfully ate her supper.

"You'd better be on your toes tomorrow," said Rankin as he passed the mashed potatoes to Dr. Beecher. "Wilson is fighting mad. He says that you've forsaken the faith."

"In what way?" asked Beecher.

"He says you're not a true Calvinist."

"Mmmm. What's he going to do about it?"

"He thinks you should be tried for heresy."

Beecher cut another slice of ham. "He's that serious?"

"Yes, Dr. Beecher, he's that serious."

"Will any of the ministers agree with him?"

"I'm afraid so. He's going to demand a vote."

"I'm not worried." Beecher stirred his coffee. "John Calvin was a mighty man of God and so was Martin Luther and Jonathan Edwards. Trouble is, some of their followers have not interpreted them correctly. But I've faced the brethren before. I'm not afraid of a trial. It will clear the air."

For the first time on the trip Calvin Stowe chuckled. "If you're tried, I want to be there," he said. "It'll be a circus. Wilson and his friends won't have a chance. The Old School is finished. A few days ago I saw the New England *primer*, which has a poem that pretty well sums up the thinking of Ashbel Green and his Old School theology. It goes like this:

'In Adam's fall
We sinned all;
In Cain's murder,
We sinned furder,
By Dr. Green,
Our sin is seen.'

"The pitiful thing is that we spend time splitting hairs

---

[2]It is estimated that by the end of slavery, 2,000 fugitives passed through the Rankin home.

while we neglect the weightier matters. Slavery, for example."

"Are you against slavery?" asked Harriet.

"Of course I'm against slavery. Still, I don't have the solution." He massaged his sideburns.

"Some of us are for colonization. Others demand immediate abolition," commented Beecher. "But I wouldn't be surprised—" he chuckled. "I wouldn't be surprised that the good Lord will provide another solution."

"Like what?" demanded Rankin.

"I really don't know. When Jesus fed the five thousand, the food was supplied by a little boy—and a miracle. That's the gospel I preach. Good works plus faith enables God to supply miracles—and solutions."

As the conversation drifted into technical theology, Harriet excused herself. "I'm tired," she said, suppressing a yawn with her hand. "I must get some rest."

Harriet had just prayed for guidance and slipped between the cool sheets when she noticed that a full moon was illuminating the land with soft, golden light. From the window she followed the Ohio as it flowed from the east to the west. Remembering the geography book she had written, she knew that the mighty stream began in Pittsburgh where the Allegheny and Monongahela united; and, growing in size, continued in a southwesterly direction to Cairo, Illinois. There it united with the mighty Mississippi and continued on to the Gulf.

As she viewed the dark ribbon below and the shadows of the hills beyond where blacks were owned and sold like cattle, she visualized Eliza crossing the ice. The black woman with a child in her arms had just reached a large chunk of ice in the center of the river when Harriet was startled by a voice.

"Now don't you worry," she heard Mrs. Rankin say. "John and I will take care of you. We'll get you to the next place in the mornin'. But aren't you hungry?"

"Yes, ma'am. We hain't had nothin' to eat fer two days."

"How many of you are there?"

"Just me and Pa."

Soon Harriet could hear the sound of utensils; then the smell of bacon and eggs drifted into her room. A couple of hours later she heard a wagon, and looking out the window, she saw John Rankin driving toward the road with the fugitives crouched on the straw in the back.

At breakfast the next morning, Harriet said, "I think you had some visitors last night."

The Rankins exchanged glances.

"What are you talking about?" asked the preacher.

Harriet related what she had heard, seen, and smelled.

"Yes, we had some visitors," agreed Mrs. Rankin. "It was an old man and his wife. Both were nearly toothless. They escaped from Tennessee and are hoping to get to Canada before winter. John took them to the next stop."

"Where's that?" asked Harriet.

"Oh, it's on the way," replied Rankin evasively.

"Then where will they go?"

"Hattie, you're asking too many questions," cautioned her father.

"That's all right," put in Rankin hurriedly. "We're all friends and we all know how to keep things under our hats. There are all kinds of stations on the Underground Railroad. Many of them are in the Cincinnati area. Most of them are so secretive that no one even knows they exist—"

"Several times when Theodore Weld and his friends were there," interrupted Beecher, "I found my horse was covered with sweat. Do you suppose that one of them might have used it to transport a slave to another station?"

"It's entirely possible," replied Rankin. "But let me tell you more about our section of Underground Railroad. An important station is in Fountain City, Indiana—about six miles north of Richmond.[3] That station is operated by Levi Coffin and his wife Catherine. Both are dedicated Quakers. They're the ones who helped Eliza after she left here.

"Even though the Quakers don't baptize or serve communion, they have done more good things for the human race than almost any denomination. They were a big help to Wilberforce in his struggle against British slavery." As he thoughtfully buttered his toast, his mood changed. Laughingly, he added, "I'll never forget an experience I had with a wonderful Quaker family. While I was visiting them, two of their daughters got into an argument. Since the one thought the other to be a little stuck-up, she shook her finger in her face and cried, 'Thee little thou thee!' "

After the laughter had quieted, he continued. "But now since I'm the moderator, I think we'd better go to the meet-

---

[3]Reconditioned, the Levi Coffin House is open for tourists.

inghouse. Dr. Wilson's probably already there!" Rising from his chair he put on his hat.

Turning to Harriet, Mrs. Rankin said, "While we're gone you can stay here and entertain yourself." She handed her a new book. "This just came last week. It's the latest biography of William Wilberforce. If you get tired of it, you might follow the path down to the river and see what a steep climb Eliza had after she had crossed the ice. I'd stay with you, but I have to help the ladies get the meal for the preachers. As you know, preachers like to eat!" She laughed. Then at the door, she said, "We'll be eating at noon and you've been invited to join us."

Harriet had read several biographies of this apparent hunchback. Most had emphasized his life-long struggle to get the transportation of slaves outlawed in the House of Commons. This book did that, but it also outlined how England got into the business of transporting slaves.

The world, Harriet learned, had been divided by Pope Alexander V1 in 1493. His *Line of Demarcation* bull barred Spain from Africa. Since Spain wanted slaves from Africa for their New World colonies, they issued *asientos* to other nations to transport slaves for them from Africa.

When the British had this license, they were as cold-blooded in supplying slaves as other nations when they had the license. Realizing that a minimum of one-third would die on the way and be tossed to the sharks, they packed their ships with enough victims so that their trip would be financially worthwhile. On a typical transport, a male slave was allotted a space six feet long by sixteen inches wide. Since the women and children were shorter, they were given less space.

Most captains arranged for their slaves to lie on their right sides "to protect their hearts." In this position, they were shackled in pairs. Handcuffs were secured to the right wrist of one and to the left wrist of his partner. Likewise, leg-irons were locked onto the left ankle of one and the right ankle of the other.

Knowing that the British public did not approve of what they were doing, the slavers developed what was known as the *Middle Passage*. This grim deception worked as follows: The public watched as the ships were being loaded with British merchandise: beads, cloth, brandy, guns, iron bars. Thus loaded, the ship sailed for Africa. There, the merchandise was

traded for slaves. Then, the captains headed for
This was the *Middle Passage.* After the slaves had b
at auction, the ship was reloaded with sugar, rum, spices.
Thus, the man-on-the-street saw British merchandise leave port, and return with products from the New World, and was supposedly unaware of what took place in the Middle Passage.

Year after year, Wilberforce fought the trade in the House of Commons. He lectured, wrote books, was defeated, started over again, continued, prayed. Sometimes his speeches were three hours long. Finally, the transportation of slaves was made illegal in 1807, a mere four years before Harriet was born.

British slaves were not actually freed until 1833. *This was just two years ago*, Harriet mused. Fortunately, Wilberforce was still alive when the final legislation was passed.

It was because of this legislation that slaves were free in Canada, and American slaves sought to get there on the Underground Railroad.

Sick and worn-out from what she had read, Harriet closed the book, put on a shawl and started down the narrow path that led to the Ohio River. Down, down she followed the goat path that twisted and turned around ravines gnawed into the surface by the elements. Once she nearly stumbled on a root that crossed the path, and several times she slipped on gravel that had worn to the surface. By the time she got to the edge of the river she was tired and out of breath.

From where she stood, she estimated the Ohio was about half a mile wide. In an effort to imagine the problems Eliza must have faced when she crossed, Harriet visualized huge chunks of ice bobbing, bumping, swirling as the winds and currents swept them toward Illinois. As a child she had often pondered over the way George Washington had crossed the Delaware that Christmas night in 1776. At the time, Washington had the advantage of a boat. Eliza had no such advantage! Instead, she had been handicapped with a child in her arms.

As Harriet daydreamed the scene and saw the desperate woman leaping, falling, getting up, and leaping and falling again, her eyes suddenly overflowed. Yes, Eliza's desire for freedom must have been overwhelming. Forcefully dismissing Eliza from her mind, she studied an isolated house or two on the opposite bank. Thinking about them, she wondered if the owners might have slaves; or if, perchance, some of them might help slaves escape by pointing them to the lantern in the Rankin house on the cliff.

Knowing that it was getting late, Harriet slowly began to climb the narrow path toward the Rankin house. Utterly exhausted when she finally got back, she faced Mrs. Rankin.

"And where have you been?" asked the lady in the apron.

"Oh, I've just been down to the river. I wanted to experience the difficulties Eliza experienced after she had crossed the ice."

"And what do you think?"

"I think she was a brave woman." Harriet shook her head. "There were so many places where she might have fallen. And she must have been dreadfully tired. Tell me, Mrs. Rankin, why did she want to escape?"

"Her master was very cruel to her. She showed me lash marks on her back that she had received from a recent beating."

"Are all masters cruel?"

"Certainly not. Many of them are very kind. After all, slaves are considered property; and who would want to damage his own property?"

"The river is so wide." Harriet's eyes brightened. "I can hardly believe that she managed to cross it," she muttered as she shook her head.

The moderator's wife tightened her apron. "The Ohio, my dear, is to the slaves what the Jordan was to the Children of Israel when they crossed over into the Promised Land. From the time they're little tots they dream about following the North Star and then crossing over into freedom. They even sing about it; and, Hattie, they're great singers. A while back a family of musical slaves knocked at our door. After we'd fed them and showed them that we'd take them to the next station, they insisted on singing to us one of their songs. I'll never forget the words. They went like this:

> Deep River, my home is over Jordan,
> Deep River, Lord, I want to cross over
> into the campground.
> Oh, don't you want to go to the Gospel feast
> That promised land, where all is peace?
> Oh, Deep River, Lord, Deep River.

"When they got through singing I was in tears. I do hope they got to Canada. Now, Hattie, my dear, it's time to eat. Let's go."

"I-I don't think I want anything to eat."

"Nonsense. We have ham, mashed potatoes, beans, cabbage, three different kinds of pie, a couple of puddings, fruit."

"N-no. I'd better stay here."

"Are you sick?"

"N-no, I'm not sick. But I can't stop thinking about Eliza and the thousands of other slaves just like her on the other side of the river. I guess my thoughts have ruined my appetite."

"I was hoping you'd go. The preachers are going to vote this afternoon on whether or not Dr. Beecher should be tried for heresy. Dr. Wilson's a very determined man. If you come along you might encourage your father."

Harriet laughed. "Pa doesn't need any encouragement. He can take care of himself. No, I'll stay here and read about Wilberforce. That small man really inspires me."

After considerable debate, it was agreed that Lyman Beecher should be tried for heresy. Undisturbed, he agreed that he would face the ministers at any time they chose, provided it didn't interfere with his schedule.

While they were bouncing back in the stage toward Cincinnati, Harriet suddenly noticed that Calvin had removed the black mourning band that had been so conspicuous just above the rim of his hat.

"What happened to the black band you were wearing?" she asked.

"Oh, I just had a visit with the Lord and He assured me that I had mourned for Eliza long enough—that I have a long life ahead of me and I should use that energy for more constructive purposes. David said, 'Weeping may endure for a night, but joy cometh in the morning' (Ps. 30:5). Notice the word 'night' is singular." A troubled smile shaped his lips.

"Even so," he continued, "I've been thinking how Eliza would have enjoyed being here—and being with you. She thought you, Hattie, were the greatest!"

"Well, I considered her a very dear friend."

"You *were* an inspiration to her. She often mentioned how she loved your writings. She said that you had a great talent for making people come alive on paper."

That evening as they stepped off the stage in Cincinnati, Calvin helped her down. Then he commented, "You remind me of Eliza."

"Which Eliza, the one who crossed the ice or your wife?"

"Both!"

"Both?" Harriet questioned.

"Yes. Your features are those of my Eliza and your determination is that of the Eliza who crossed the ice. Your indomitable determination must come from all those blacksmiths in the Beecher line."

Facing each other, they laughed.

"Incidentally, will you be at the Semi-Colon Club next Monday?" he asked.

"I certainly will," she replied with animation.

"Then I'll see you there?"

"Yes, you'll see me there," agreed Harriet.

15

Romance!

Hours before it was time to leave, Harriet selected her best Sunday dress, the long black one with lace at the collar and fringes of lace at the ends of the arm-length sleeves. After ironing it, she carefully combed and tightened the five curls on each side of her head.

Standing before the mirror, she smiled at herself. As an afterthought she put a touch of perfume behind each ear. Being an hour ahead of time, she tried to outline a story about Eliza crossing on the ice. The words didn't flow. She wrote, rewrote, crossed out. She couldn't even think of a first sentence. And the minutes seemed to merely creep by. She wound the clock to make certain that it was running.

Harriet was the first to arrive at the Semi-Colon Club. "I hear my brother-in-law is about to be tried for heresy," said Uncle Samuel after he had greeted her.

"That's right. It's Dr. Wilson's idea."

"Are you worried?"

"Worried about Pa? Never! He knows more about the ins and outs of theology than anyone in America. He used to practice on us while we were stacking wood. The Five Points of Calvinism and all their problems are as familiar to him as the palm of his hand. And he's a great debater. He loves a church fight."

While they were talking, Calvin Stowe strode in and took a seat behind her. "What's on the program?" he asked.

"Nothing to be excited about," replied Samuel. "Salmon Chase was going to tell us how to look up obscure legal points in the law, but he's tied up with another runaway case."

After Sam Foote had disappeared, Calvin said, "I came early because Dr. Beecher asked me to preach a series of sermons on the origin of the Bible. I'm excited, since that's my field. He assured me that if someone will record excerpts of my sermons, they'll be printed in the Cincinnati paper. Do you know anyone who might help?"

"I'd be glad to help," offered Harriet quickly.

"Great. But it might be a good idea if we could meet together before the services so you'll know better what to write. Some of my material will be a little complicated."

"We could meet in Papa's study."

"Fine. I want to do a good job. Lane has had enough bad publicity. Maybe we could help turn things around."

Neither Harriet nor Calvin paid much attention to the program that followed nor did they stay for refreshments. Calvin walked her home, taking the longest route.

Several weeks after the series was completed, a teacher friend invited Harriet to go with her to Kentucky. Traveling eastward on the Ohio, they stopped at Maysville and then continued a dozen miles south to Washington where they visited a plantation. There, they were received as guests in the comfortable "Big House." Harriet was fascinated. Here was slavery at its best. She saw the little cabins where the slaves stayed, noticed their private gardens, heard them singing and laughing as they worked. She also visited nearby plantations. At one of them she watched a little boy dance, do imitations, sing, make faces and entertain the whites who came to watch. On a Sunday, she visited a church in a small town. In her book, *A Key to Uncle Tom's Cabin*, Harriet described the occasion:

My "attention was called to a beautiful quadroon girl, who sat in one of the slips of the church, and appeared to have charge of some young children. . . . When [I] returned from the church [I] enquired about the girl, and was told that she was as good and amiable as she was beautiful; that she was a pious girl, and a member of the church; and finally that she was *owned* by Mr. So-and-so. The idea that this girl was a slave struck a chill to [my] heart, and [I] said earnestly, 'Oh, I hope they treat her kindly!' "

"Oh, certainly!" was the reply; "they think as much of her as their own children."

"I hope they will never sell her," said a person in the company.

"Certainly they will not; a southern gentleman, not long ago, offered her master a thousand dollars for her; but he told him that she was too good to be his wife, and he certainly should not have her for his mistress."[1]

Her mind filled with scenes she would never forget, Harriet returned to Cincinnati. Soon she learned that her father would be tried for heresy within a few weeks. The trial, she knew, could have severe consequences. If he were found guilty, he would have to resign from Lane; and, being nearly penniless, that would mean he would be destitute. But he seemed unconcerned, although he frequently brought up the problem at mealtime.

"If a man," he often said, "cannot obey the law of God, why should he try? It is fatalism to say, 'If God chooses to save me, I'll be saved—if He doesn't, I'll be lost. One way or another, I can do nothing about it.' " This state of mind, he contended while thumping the table with his fist, is letting "the bottom fall out of accountability."

It was his feeling that part of his task in life was to restore the doctrine of man's accountability. He believed in the possibility of immediate repentance and that man could repent of his own free will and then, by God's grace, be saved. Jesus, he insisted, died for all.

On the day of the trial, Harriet sat in the back of the church. As she was praying, Henry Ward joined her. Calvin Stowe took a seat in front. In his autobiography, Lyman Beecher described the occasion.

> When the trial came on, I took all my books and sat down on the second stair of the pulpit. It was my church. I looked so quiet and meek my students were almost afraid I shouldn't come up to the mark. I had everything just then to weigh me down. My wife was lying at home on her dying bed. She did not live a fortnight after that. Then there was all the wear and tear of the seminary and of my congregation. But when I had all my references and had nothing to do but extemporize, I felt easy. I had as much lawyer about me as Wilson and more. I never got into a corner and he never got out, though the fact is he made as good a case as could be made on the wrong side. . . .[2]

As the trial droned on with an occasional flurry of sparks, Harriet was proud of her father. He proved that he was correct

[1]A *Key to Uncle Tom's Cabin*, p. 41.
[2]*Autobiography*. Vol. 2, pp. 351–352.

when he boasted, "I know to a hair's-breadth every point between the Old School and the New School." But even though he was acquitted by a vote of twenty-three to twelve, Dr. Wilson announced that he was appealing the case to the Synod, which was scheduled to meet in Dayton that October.

The moment the meeting was dismissed, Calvin Stowe rushed up to Harriet. "I knew your father would win!" he exclaimed, taking both her hands in his. "He has a great mind—and he knows the facts."

"But what about the appeal?" asked Harriet nervously.

"That's nothing to worry about. He'll win again." He patted her shoulder. "Yes, he'll win again."

Harriet visited her stepmother as frequently as possible. But her illness, which had started several months before, took a turn for the worse immediately after the trial. On a Thursday afternoon, after she had had a visit with her, Harriet had a long talk with Henry Ward.

"What do you think of Professor Stowe?" she asked.

"He's the best professor in the entire seminary; and he knows more about the origin of the books of the Bible than anyone alive. He was the valedictorian of all his classes. Franklin Pierce [President of the United States, 1853–1857] says that the only reason he made good grades at Bowdoin was because he always sat next to Calvin Stowe when examinations were given." He laughed. "But why do you ask?"

"We've been together a lot lately, and I don't want to make a mistake—"

"It wouldn't be a mistake to marry him. He's a great and good man. But like Pa he's a hypochondriac and when he gets the blues he gets the blues. Sometimes he even has to go to bed because of the blues. He also loses his hat and he's completely impracticable about ordinary things. And he likes to eat. In fact, he'll eat anything in sight."

Harriet Porter Beecher died on July 7. She was buried next to Eliza Stowe on the seminary campus. After Harriet had placed flowers on her stepmother's grave, she left her father and accompanied Calvin to Eliza's grave. She had been dead for nearly a year. Harriet's heart especially went out to the now motherless children of her stepmother. James was seven, Thomas thirteen, and Isabella fifteen.

A bright glow softened the sorrow in the Beecher home a month later. All of the eleven Beecher children decided to have a grand get-together in Cincinnati. It was a great time for Lyman Beecher since his children had never been together before; and Mary had never even seen little Jamie.

Each of the children had glowing reports about what they were doing. Edward was colorfully articulate, for he had just succeeded in getting a charter for his Illinois college from the state legislature. "One member who fought me," he said, "liked to boast that he was 'born in a briar thicket, rocked in a hog trough, and had never had his genius cramped by the pestilential air of a college.'[3] That fellow was as tough as Old Hickory himself. But there was another member I really liked. He was a tall, thin man by the name of Abraham Lincoln. Abe was always full of stories."

"I knew you'd succeed," beamed Lyman. "I've never forgotten how when you were going to Yale, you used to spend Saturday night in Litchfield, sing in the choir, have Sunday dinner with us, and then, packing a knapsack, walk all the way back to New Haven and recite in a class on Monday morning." He shook his head. "I never knew how you managed it."

"The night air was good for me," replied Edward.

"It must have been. You were the valedictorian of your class."

The Beecher clan had a great time. They teased. Laughed. Boasted. Henry Ward, with the help of Samuel P. Chase, had founded the Young Men's Temperance Society; Catherine's geography book (with ghost writer Harriet!) had sold 100,000 copies; and Harriet was writing and selling numerous articles.

On Sunday Lyman Beecher was proud to have his sons take the Sunday services in the Second Presbyterian Church. Edward preached in the morning, William H. in the afternoon, and George in the evening. And during each service the Beecher clan filled the first three rows.

The newspaper had a glowing report of the three-day session:

> Monday morning they assembled, and, after reading and prayers, in which all joined, they formed a circle. The doctor stood in the middle and gave them a thrilling speech. He then went round and gave them each a kiss. They had a happy dinner.
>
> Presents flowed in from all quarters. During the afternoon the house was filled with company, each bringing an

---

[3]Saints, Sinners and Beechers, p. 147.

> offering. When left alone at evening, they had a general examination of their characters. The shafts of wit flew. The doctor being struck in several places; he was, however, expert enough to hit most of them in turn. From the uproar of the general battle, all must have been wounded.
>
> Tuesday morning saw them together again, drawn up in a straight line for the inspection of the king of happy men. After receiving particular instructions, they formed into a circle. The doctor made a long and affecting speech. He felt that he stood for the last time in the midst of all his children, and each word fell with the weight of a patriarch's. He embraced them once more in the tenderness of his big heart. Each took of all a farewell kiss. With hands joined, they sang a hymn. A prayer was offered, and, finally, a parting blessing was spoken. Thus ended a meeting which can only be rivaled in that blessed home where the ransomed of the Lord, after weary pilgrimage, shall join in the praise of the Lamb.[4]

From his stand on top of Mt. Pisgah, Lyman Beecher viewed the future. He was profoundly satisfied with the progress of his children; but he was disturbed by darkening clouds moving in from the east. He wondered about the future of Lane, of his children—and of himself. He knew he would soon be heading for his heresy trial in Dayton; and he also knew that his fellow pastor, Joshua Lacy Wilson, encouraged by voices from Princeton, was determined to nail him to the wall.

The time of the trial arrived and, accompanied by Henry Ward and Charles, Lyman took his seat in a canal boat and headed for Dayton. Letters from Henry Ward to the family in Cincinnati provide a glimpse of what took place. Being young and caustic, he wrote: "I never saw so many faces of clergymen—and so few of them intelligent."

During the trial, which lasted nearly a week, Lyman Beecher knew he faced a packed jury. This was because none of the ministers from the Cincinnati Presbytery were allowed to vote. But remembering that Paganini had moved an audience with merely a G string, and convinced that he was right, this son and grandson of blacksmiths was not unduly worried.

Beecher listened with great patience as Wilson denounced him. Then Lyman stood to his feet. Again he was "old man eloquent." Still the Big Gun of Calvinism, he fired, reloaded, and kept firing until he could see by the faces of his former

---

[4]*Crusader in Crinoline*, p. 159.

opposition that he had won them over.

The vote was ten to one in Beecher's favor. When the verdict was announced, Dr. Wilson turned pale. This was because, according to the Book of Discipline, if an accuser failed to prove his accusation, he himself could be subjected to trial as a slanderer of a fellow minister.

After Calvin had explained to Harriet some of the more subtle points in the hair-splitting that had taken place in her dad's trial in Dayton, he drew her close. "Hattie," he said soberly, "I have something I want to share with you tonight. It's extremely important and I think we ought to be alone. Do you think we could go somewhere for dinner at around seven o'clock."

"I was planning to write an article. But, yes, I think I can make it," she replied.

That afternoon as she ironed her dress and refashioned her curls, she wondered what he had in mind. In recent weeks their meetings together had increased in length and in number. And once he had accidentally used the word 'dear.' *Was he going to bare his heart? And if he did, what would be her response?*

Sitting opposite from Calvin in a private cove in a moderately expensive restaurant was a new experience. Across the candle-lit table, tastefully set with costly silver, he began. "I have something important to share with you. Do you remember when I gave those lectures on the origin of the Bible?"

"How could I ever forget? I learned more from you and in writing up the lectures for the paper than I had ever learned about the Bible. You really opened my eyes." She leaned forward.

"The Bible *is* a most fascinating library, and you were a big help. I couldn't have—" Calvin smiled with satisfaction.

He was interrupted by the appearance of the waiter, a tall black man in a blue coat featuring two rows of brass buttons. "Our specialty today is catfish," he said, flashing two rows of sparkling white teeth.

"Sounds good to me," responded Calvin.

"I've never eaten catfish, but I'll try it," agreed Harriet.

After they had chosen between soup and salad and had selected their vegetables, Calvin asked, "Do you have religious scruples against catfish?"

"Oh no. I've just never eaten catfish. Are there those who have religious scruples against it?"

"Of course."

"Why?"

"Because in the eleventh chapter of Leviticus Moses taught the people that they should eat nothing from the seas or the rivers that didn't have scales and fins. Catfish have fins, but they don't have scales."

"Then why are we eating catfish?"

"Because in the eleventh chapter of Acts our friend Simon Peter revealed that he had had a vision from the Lord in which he was instructed not to call such things unclean."

"That means that we have scriptural support for eating catfish?"

"Yes, we can eat catfish and shrimp and even lobster without being heretics, and lobsters have neither fins nor scales!"

They both laughed.

As they proceeded with the meal, Harriet kept wondering when Calvin was going to bring up the "important subject." Finally, as they were eating apple pie topped with ice cream, Calvin withdrew a thick envelope from his pocket. Opening it, he said, "Hattie, you did such a good job reporting my lectures, Corey, Fairbank & Webster are going to bring them out in a book. This is the contract. The book will be titled *Introduction to the Criticism and Interpretation of the Bible*."

"Congratulations," replied Harriet, forcing a smile. "I hope you follow it with many other books. Your knowledge should be spread on paper."

"Actually, Hattie, you're a much better writer then I am. You think in pictures. I think in facts."

"An ideal writer should think in both facts and pictures."

Calvin stirred his coffee. "True, but we're all different. However, there is a way that such a person might be made."

"How?" Harriet asked.

"It's a biblical way." A tiny smile tugged at his lips.

"Explain."

"Jesus said, 'For this cause shall a man leave his father and mother, and cleave to his wife; and they twain shall be one flesh" (Mark 10:7–8).

"What do you mean?"

"You think in pictures. I think in facts—"

"And when shall we go about making such a person?"

"How about the first week of January?"

"The first week of January will be fine even though there will be snowdrifts, icicles, slippery roads, and cakes of ice in the Ohio."

"What do you mean?" asked Calvin.

"Oh, I'm just thinking in pictures!" Harriet smiled.

"The date, then, will be January 6. I've checked the calendar and Hattie, my dear, that is the most convenient date. I always consider the facts!"

They both burst out laughing. As he took her hands in his, Harriet could hardly believe that at last she had found someone who loved her and thought she was special. After finishing the meal, they continued to discuss the future—their writing, his children and her new responsibility. She was confident about her future role since she herself had had a stepmother and enjoyed a warm relationship.

Harriet's engagement was kept secret for a long time, even from the family. But both Harriet and Calvin counted the days, then the hours, and then the minutes when the one who was dominated by facts would be united with the one who was dominated by pictures—a union forming a unique person.

The wedding day arrived, with some trepidation on Harriet's part. Dressed in her finest, and with her curls freshly formed, Harriet stepped into her father's home. Upon her arrival, she learned that Calvin had not yet appeared. Still, it was early, and Harriet knew that he, the fact-loving man, never did anything until the last split second. While hoping he would appear on time, she trusted that he would not faint during the ceremony as did Salmon P. Chase.

While she waited, Harriet scribbled a note to Georgiana:

> Well, my dear G., about half an hour more and your old friend, companion, schoolmate, etc., will cease to be Hattie Beecher and change to nobody knows who. Since you are engaged and pledge in a year or two to encounter a similar fate, do you wish to know how you shall feel? Well, I have been dreading and dreading the time. I lay awake all last week wondering how I should live through this overwhelming crisis, and lo! it has come, and I feel *nothing at all*.
>
> The wedding is to be altogether domestic—nobody present but my own brothers and sisters, and my old colleague, Mary Dutton; and as there is sufficiency of the ministry in our family we do not have to call in the foreign aid of a minister. . . .
>
> Well, here comes Mr. S., so farewell, and for the last time I subscribe,
>
> Your own
> H.E.B.

Curiously, Harriet did not immediately mail that note. Was it because of the expensive postage—25¢ a sheet? Or was it because she was upset by an ad that appeared in a Cincinnati paper a few weeks before? That ad in the *Republican* read:

$1000 REWARD

RAN AWAY from the Subscriber, on Saturday the 12th instant, December, 1835

ELEVEN SLAVES

First, DANIEL, aged about 55; ABBE, his wife, about 50; and their children: Daniel, about 25; Adam, about 22; Jonathan, about 21; Anthony, about 20; Judy, about 19; William, about 16; James, about 11; Ruben, about 10; Moses, about 9.

The above Slaves are all remarkably likely Negroes—light complexioned, tall, and of fine appearance, and no doubt well-dressed and independent in their appearance, having been much indulged by me. I will give the above reward of One Thousand dollars for the delivery of the above family of Slaves to me, or the securing of them in any jail, either in or out of the state, so that I can get them. Or I will give One Hundred dollars for the securing and delivery of each one of them, and pay all reasonable expenses incurred in the delivery of them.

JAMES TAYLOR
Newport, Ky.

In spite of that disturbing news, Harriet set her mind on new ventures. She and Calvin had a good and loving relationship.

Toward the end of January, after Harriet had settled in her new home—probably the one in which Calvin and Eliza had lived—Harriet picked up her unmailed note and added several pages. This is the opening paragraph:

> Three weeks have passed since writing the above, and my husband and self are now quietly settled by our fireside; as domestic as any pair of tame fowl. . . . Two days after our marriage we took a wedding excursion, though we would have most gladly been excused this conformity had not necessity required Mr. Stowe to visit Columbus. . . .

The reason Stowe was "required" to go to Columbus was

to address the Western College of Teachers on *Prussian Education*. It so happened that General William Harrison, hero of the Battle of Tippecanoe, was in the audience. He—elected President of the United States in 1840—was so impressed by Stowe's thesis, he helped fulfill one of Lyman's fondest dreams.

Lane Seminary needed books—thousands of books. Since many of the needed books originated in Europe, Calvin, fluent in several European languages, was the ideal person to select them. But where would the struggling school get the money to send him? Harrison helped arrange for the state legislature to supply part of that need.

Plans having been made for Calvin to go on a book-buying tour, Harriet picked up her pen to add a few more lines to the first double spurts of writing which had not been mailed. She wrote:

> Dear Georgy, naughty girl that I am, it is a month that I have let the above lie by, because I got into a strain of emotion in it that I dreaded to return to. Well, it shall be no longer. In about five weeks Mr. Stowe and myself start for New England. He sails the first of May. I am going with him to Boston, New York, and other places, and shall stop finally at Hartford, whence, as soon as he is gone, it is my intention to turn westward.

Why didn't Harriet sail with him? London, Vienna, Florence, Venice, Rome were cities she longed to visit. She couldn't go, for she had learned that in due time she would become a mother.

On their final day together, neither realized the troubles that they, Lane Seminary, and the city of Cincinnati would soon be facing. Had they known about those troubles, he would not have sailed.

16
Trail of Tears

Struggling with tears, Harriet began the long journey back to Cincinnati alone. Her nearly four months of marriage had been a continuing and ever-increasing ecstasy. And now *he* was gone!

Parallels between Calvin Stowe and Alexander Fisher kept wedging into her mind. Both were brilliant. Both were dominated by worthy purpose. Both had sailed to Europe in the spring. Alas, Fisher had gone down with the ship off the coast of Ireland. Harriet still remembered the day her father had received the sad news and relayed it to Catherine. For months afterward Catherine had been so broken-hearted she had longed to die.

Again and again Harriet prayed, "Oh, Lord, protect Calvin in every way. Help him fulfill the purpose of this trip. Shield him from every temptation. And, dear Lord, help me carry this child that is growing beneath my heart. May it, whether it is a boy or girl, grow up to serve Thee and Thy purpose."

Since the home she and Calvin were building was far from completion, Harriet moved in with her father and the children by his second wife along with his other relatives. She kept busy making and repairing clothes for the children, helping them with their lessons, writing an occasional article or story—and keeping a stream of letters flowing to Calvin. Calvin liked news; and since Cincinnati was brimming with news, she kept him well informed.

That April, about a month before Calvin sailed, a white boy and a black boy got into a fight. A riot developed and several blacks were killed. Then while Cincinnati seethed with rumors, James G. Birney, the rich abolitionist from Alabama who called on Catherine in Hartford for advice in starting a school for women in Huntsville, moved into the city. There, he set up his abolitionist paper, the *Philanthropist*. Soon his presses were turning out copy that was sent all across the country. Confident that few would object, Birney hired Dr. Gamaliel Bailey, a young surgeon in the Cincinnati Hospital, to be his assistant editor.

Bailey, a devout Methodist, worked hard. The paper denounced slavery in every issue. Harriet watched—and wondered; and as the days passed the modest grumblings of opposition became a roar. Soon, Jacob Burnet, a deacon in Beecher's church and a judge on the Ohio Supreme Court, led a committee that called on James Birney.

"The people in Cincinnati don't like your paper," said the judge. "Take my advice and close down."

"What if I refuse?" asked Birney.

"There will be a riot. Houses will be burned. People will be killed."

"But isn't Ohio a free state?"

"It is free. But every July southern planters come to Cincinnati on their semiannual buying trip. Their business is our mainstay. Free or not, our merchants need business. The south loathes your paper. . . . You're sitting on a keg of dynamite. The fuse, Mr. Birney, is extremely short; and there are many radicals anxious to touch it with a flame."

Both Birney and Bailey merely smiled.

On July 12 a mob broke into the printing shop of Achilles Pugh—the antislavery Quaker who was brave enough to print the *Philanthropist*. While substantial citizens looked on without saying a word, they damaged both the press and the type that was all set ready to print.

Undaunted, the editors repaired the damage and the *Philanthropist* appeared on schedule.

Swollen with child, Harriet wondered what would happen next. Her father was in Pittsburgh facing his third heresy trial. Fortunately for her morale, Henry Ward was near. Better yet, Henry Ward had access to a brace of pistols.

Samuel Davis, the newly elected mayor who had campaigned on a law-and-order ticket, printed a notice and posted it in almost every public place. His notice offered $100 to anyone who could secure the arrest and conviction of any member of the mob. The next day startled citizens noticed that the mayor's bulletin had been replaced by another which

Todd, Charles Burr. *In Olde Connecticut*. Grafton Press, 1906.

Wagenknecht, Edward. *Harriet Beecher Stowe*. Oxford University Press, 1965.

Wilson, Forrest. *Crusader in Crinoline*. J. B. Lippincott, 1941.

Wilson, Francis. *John Wilkes Booth*. Houghton Mifflin, 1929.